A CLASSIC TRAGEDY: SHORT STORIES

Xu Xiaobin is an influential and prolific Chinese female writer of fictions, proses and scripts. Born in Beijing, Xu started to publish literary works in 1981. Xu is noted for writings of searing emotional honesty about gender and sexuality, that push the boundaries of what is politically acceptable in today's China. Her works include magnum opus *Feathered Serpent* (1998 novel), *Dream of Dunhuang* (1994 novel), *Princess Deling* (2004 novel) and *Pisces* (1995 novella). A winner of a number of renowned literary awards, such as Lu Xun Literature Prize and China's National Literary Creative Writing Award, Xu's masterpieces have been translated into English, French, German, Italian, Japanese, Spanish, Portuguese, Korean, Norwegian and other languages.

Natascha Bruce translates fiction, creative non-fiction and poetry from Chinese. Her work includes *Lonely Face* by Yeng Pway Ngon (shortlisted for the TA First Translation Prize) and *Lake Like a Mirror* by Ho Sok Fong (shortlisted for the Warwick Prize for Women in Translation). She is the recipient of a 2020 PEN/Heim Translation Fund Grant for the translation of *Owlish* by Dorothy Tse.

Nicky Harman lives in the UK and is a full-time translator of Chinese literary works. She has won several awards, including the 2020 Special Book Award of China, the 2015 Mao Tai Cup People's Literature Chinese-English translation prize, and the 2013 China International Translation Contest, Chinese-to-English section. When not translating, she promotes contemporary Chinese fiction literary events through teaching, blogs, talks and her work on Paper-Republic.org.

Balestier Press
Centurion House, London TW18 4AX
www.balestier.com

A Classic Tragedy: Short Stories
Copyright © Xu Xiaobin, 2012
English translation copyright © Natascha Bruce and Nicky Harman, 2021

Originally published in Chinese in 2012 by Writers Publishing House, Beijing
Original titles: 天籁, 古典悲剧, 花瓣儿, 亚姐, 银盾,
过门儿, 黄和平, 美术馆, 密钥的故事, 黑瀑

First published in English by Balestier Press in 2021

Cover illustration by Xu Xiaobin

A CIP catalogue record for this book
is available from the British Library.

ISBN 978-1-911221-28-9

This book is a work of fiction. The literary perceptions and
insights are based on experience; all names, characters, places,
and incidents either are products of the author's imagination
or are used fictitiously.

Xu Xiaobin

A CLASSIC TRAGEDY: SHORT STORIES

Translated from the Chinese by

Natascha Bruce and Nicky Harman

BALESTIER PRESS

LONDON · SINGAPORE

Contents

A Celestial Voice

Everyone living on Pine Crag had always known about the healing springs, where the waters were a translucent sapphire blue, a poisonous blue. They were said to be the eyes of the Immortal Maiden, so no one dared touch them.

Then a couple of years ago, the springs were developed into a spa. That was down to one woman, all the Pine Crag folk knew that. Her name was Suisui. She had started out as just another Pine Crag girl, but was re-christened the Empress of Flower Songs when she was invited to Beijing to sing on a CCTV late show. After her 'flower songs', as they were called, the whole world knew that Suisui came from Pine Crag. And everyone knew it was the Pine Crag folk who were the first to discover Suisui, and the healing springs.

The locals spoke as they saw: Suisui was no ordinary girl, they insisted. She was the beauty of Pine Crag. Her skin had a natural blush, like a water lily bud about to burst into summer bloom, and her long hair, caught back in a ponytail and swishing across her slender back, was like silk cogon grass. And then there were those eyebrows, those lips, her naturally fine features. Only her eyes had something odd about them: although they were as shapely as those of any girl in a Yangliuqing folk painting, they were dull and slow-moving, and as murky as spring waters enveloped in mist – Suisui was blind.

The Pine Crag folk did not see her as blind, the same way that, with the passing of time, they did not see the springs as particularly blue. They just knew that she sang beautifully, like the spring waters on a snowy day, with a pure golden warmth, clear as a bell. At the age of eight, Suisui learnt to sing the flower song which goes:

> *There's nothing rounder than the moon,*
> *Nothing squarer than a grain scoop,*
> *Nothing prettier than a bright bridal garland;*
> *Nothing handsomer than his body,*
> *Nothing softer than her hands,*
> *Nothing lovelier than the finest flower songs…*
> *A little moon hangs at the window,*
> *The moonlight shines on the kang,*
> *The little mandarin ducks alight on the pillow,*
> *The golden phoenix falls on the quilt.*

Her singing made the work team leader cry so hard that she forgot to wipe away the tears that rolled down her cheeks. As the song finished, she said: 'How can such a little lass sing so movingly? So young and it's as if her heart is bleeding!' Suisui had not yet gone blind, and she had brilliant phoenix eyes, the whites almost the blue of the waters of the healing springs.

The work team leader wanted Suisui to take the exam for the county song and dance troupe. She knew that the girl's mother had been bringing up Suisui on her own for years and that the two were very close, so she worried that the mother might not let her go, but to her surprise, she agreed with alacrity. In fact, her eyes sparkled with excitement and she looked ten years younger.

But a few days later, Suisui was back, having failed to get a place. The reason was not that she was no good as a singer, but that she had failed to take the exam. On their way to the exam hall, the work team leader had bought her two lamb kebabs, the roasted chunks of meat gleaming with rich yellow globules of fat. 'Nice?' asked the team leader. Suisui nodded wordlessly as she munched on her kebab. And then she disappeared.

The work team leader shouted herself hoarse, and even put out an announcement on the town loudspeaker system, but it was only towards evening that one of the supermarket salesgirls brought Suisui back. By that time, the exams were long over.

Neither of them spoke on the journey home. Suisui's head was full of the delights of the supermarket – it was the first time in her life that she had been in one, and there were so many multi-coloured tins, all so pretty. The prettiest was the tin with a picture of a big white pig on it, such a gentle creature! It reminded her of the boiled pork in garlic paste that her mother used to make. It was a very long time since they had had that at home. The translucent pieces of fatty pork melted in your mouth, and Suisui could easily eat a whole bowlful at one go. Suisui was the kind of kid who never put on weight. Her mother chided her for eating so much, but she was secretly pleased; Suisui was just born that way, a child who never got fat when she ate pork and never got thin when she only had pickles with her dinner. She could have been brought up in a midden but she was like a lotus root, one rinse in water, and she scrubbed up to a pure tender white. That was just the way she was!

But when they arrived home that day, this once-proud mother bawled her daughter out so loudly that the whole of Pine Crag heard: 'Useless girl! Can't you do anything right? So the tins looked pretty, does that make them yours? You spent the whole afternoon wandering round some lousy supermarket? What a simpleton you are! The Lord God gave you a voice of gold and this is how you waste it! What use are eyes to a singer? Pretty, indeed! If I had my way, you'd never see anything ever again!'

The threat, shouted at the top of her voice, terrified the entire village. It wasn't good to say things like that, muttered the elders, shaking their heads. And, sure enough, a few days later, Suisui's mother appeared, her face red from weeping, and told them that Suisui had had a fever and lost the sight in both eyes. The elders reassured her that this happened when children had a high fever, and her daughter would be fine in a few days, but the woman carried on shaking her head and crying, and Suisui never did get her sight back.

Suisui was still so little that she wasn't worried. After all, she had her mum to look after her, and make sure she never went short of food or clothes. If she wanted boiled pork in garlic paste, her mother would go five *li* to buy fresh pork, scald it in boiling water to drain off the blood, pound up garlic, fine salt and monosodium glutamate, and then add a few drops of chili oil that glistened red against the pale meat. Indescribably delicious, and all for Suisui: her mother would not touch a single morsel, just sat watching her daughter devouring a whole bowlful, then washed up after her.

The observant in the village noticed how much older Suisui's mother was looking.

Suisui's mother was not actually from Pine Crag. She was a city girl, sent there during one of the political campaigns. Rumour had it that she used to be a crooner back home, but no one here had ever heard her sing. Apart from the one time she bawled Suisui out, she never raised her voice to anyone. But no one was denying that she was educated. Whenever the villagers needed couplets written at the Chinese New Year, it was always her they went to. And education earned respect. Pine Crag was so very poor that it was only Suisui's generation who could expect to complete primary school. Suisui's mother stood out head and shoulders above the other villagers, respected even by the elders of the local township.

Going blind certainly ensured that Suisui concentrated on her singing, and it was after her accident that she really began to excel, or so said the villagers. Every evening, as they packed up and put their tools away, they would hear her voice soaring from the high mountain top, where she got her mother to take her so she could sing. Her voice had lost its childish sweetness, and there was something poignant in the bright clear notes, something bleak amid the sweetness, and a depth that none of the other folk singers had.

The first month comes and it's Spring, oh!
Red lanterns hang from the courtyard gate
You can ask up and down the village,
They'll all say I don't fancy you.

The second month comes and the dragon looks up, oh!
Third sister Wang will toy with a bridal garland
With no one around, I'll take your hand
If someone comes, you hide back there.

The third month comes, and on the third day, oh!
The Queen Mother of the West has her birthday
Our beloved girl sits on the ground
Singing her youth away.

The fourth month comes and peonies bloom
Little sister's eyes are plucked out
The young man, oh, he goes away
Leaving his lover behind.

The fifth of the fifth, it's the Dragon Boat feast
Let's drink ruby wine, oh!

Let's open King Yama's Roll of the Dead
You and I are fated to stay together.

The sixth month comes, oh, and five red waves
I wash my clothes in clear water
I miss you by day, dream of you by night
I cry enough tears to flood a gully.

The workers coming home from the fields used to applaud but shake their heads too. 'Strange girl, so full of emotions!' And tears rolled down the cheeks of the elders when they heard her sing the line, 'Little sister's eyes are plucked out...' 'I feel sorry for Suisui's mother,' they said. 'She beat her daughter blind, and we haven't seen her smile since. Her eyes are always puffed up like rotten peaches!'

And so Suisui grew up amid flower songs, and she was as lovely as a flower herself. When the Cultural Revolution ended and the first flower songfest was held, everyone in Pine Crag, young and old alike, put Suisui's name forward, but she was too young to compete. Meantime, every young village woman with a decent voice plastered her cheeks with rouge and donned the dress she kept for high days and holidays. The day of the gathering, singers from seven of the local townships converged on the banks of Pine Crag River, where the wild peonies had just come into bloom. Pine Crag was famous for its wild peonies, which clothed its hillsides in brilliant pinks and purples, like glorious sunset clouds.

There was a story attached to the flower songfest: many years before, a huntsman had apparently passed by during the peony blossom season, and seen a beautiful young woman singing as she bathed herself in the waters of the healing springs. The young man was instantly captivated by her soft voice and the soaring notes of her song. He never saw the woman again, though he looked everywhere for her, but he never forgot the song. The locals all said she must have been a goddess descended from the heavens, and they erected a temple to her at the foot of Pine Crag. Every year on the anniversary of the huntsman's sighting – that was the twenty-eighth day of the fourth month of the lunar calendar – they gathered there to sing the song the goddess had bequeathed to them. They also gave Pine Crag the name 'Song Mountain'.

This year the songfest was particularly lively and, as if in response, the wild peonies were truly spectacular. The bright colours of the women's dresses mingled with the flowers, and the songs were fresh and new:

Boy:
> *In the trees, the little birds cheep, oh!*
> *Hearts a-flutter, eyelids a-quiver*
> *Last night, I dreamed of you, oh!*
> *Today you smiled at me.*

Girl:
> *The lambkin climbs the southern mountain, oh!*
> *The huntsmen chase behind*
> *You have eaten your way into my heart, oh!*
> *By day and by night, I think of you…*

One handsome young man from Linjiazhai village sang for several hours, duetting with the young women, and as each woman, one after another conceded defeat, it seemed he would be crowned the Emperor of Song.

Finally, Suisui stepped to the front of the ranks of the gaudy Pine Crag singers, looking for all the world like a goddess descended to earth in her plain white dress.

The young man from Linjiazhai village was singing:

> *Eighteen plum deer cross the mountain peak*
> *Young huntsman follows behind*
> *He is the honeybee, his girl is the flower*
> *The honeybee stings the flesh of the flower.*

A young Pine Crag woman responded:

> *The fawns come down from the mountain, oh!*
> *Come down to drink some water, oh!*
> *The man I love comes to me, oh!*
> *Grips my small hand and sings, oh!*

The young man sang back:

> *Yang Wulang became a monk on Mount Wutaishan*
> *Zhuge Liang went down the Four Rivers*
> *A young girl sits on the ground, plucking grass*
> *Flowers are her gift for this young man.*

The young woman could think of nothing to follow with and, cheeks aflame, gazed around her. Just at that moment, Suisui stepped towards her, and the young woman shoved her forward. Suisui was quite unafraid. She had been a bashful child but there was no trace of that left now. She was as bold as could be, and let rip with her voice, as if to pierce the darkness in front of her:

> *In the soybean fields, a potato plant flowers*
> *Three years in a row, the flowers bear no fruit.*
> *Young man, do not laugh at my song,*
> *This lass has only just left home.*

She was greeted with cheers as she finished. She sang each word with such determination, flinging them forth in the song. Fired up by Suisui's charm and beauty, the young man took up anew:

> *Eighteen mules walk through Jingyang county*
> *Which is the most reliable?*
> *This lass is so good-looking*
> *Which village does she come from?*

Suisui may have lost her sight, but her hearing was extraordinarily acute. She could hear the guy's singing was a bit different from the way a Pine Crag youth would sing, and guessed also he was well-known, so in the next verse she upped her game:

> *Eighteen mules walk through Jingyang county*
> *The lead mule is the most reliable*
> *This lass is a young fern frond*
> *This girl is from Pine Crag village.*

Emboldened, the young man sang back:

> *Jingyang straw hats turned eighteen times*
> *A crimson waist-tie turned twice around*
> *One born handsome, one grows pretty*
> *This lass is like a just-opened peony*

Suisui showed no signs of tempering her lyrics, they fairly sizzled:

> *Jingyang straw hats, you put yours on, oh!*
> *Or the Pine Crag rain might wet you*

Young man, this lass loves you
Which village is your talent from?

By now, all the other singers had stopped and were listening quietly to the repartee between these two. The TV crew walked over hefting their equipment and pointed it at them. This embarrassed the young guy but had no effect on Suisui, who could not see, so continued to sing as naturally as ever.

That day they sang until the sun set behind the mountains. As the light faded, no one moved. Everyone was quiet, there was no more applause. Suisui's hair streamed out in the evening breeze, which carried the songs to her listeners. They were transfixed, moved to silent tears at the sight of this beautiful, sightless girl. Two weeks later, the TV crew were back, and took Suisui and her mother away with them.

When they arrived in Beijing, Suisui was distressed by not being able to see for the first time. One day her mother took her shopping, determined to find her daughter something decent to wear. As Suisui ran her hands over the silk dresses, slippery, fine and cool to the touch, she felt as if she was in a dream. They were all lovely. Her mother described them: this one is crimson, this one is dark yellow, this one is olive-green, and this one is a white check on blue. 'Which do you want?' she asked. 'You choose, Mum,' said Suisui. 'Whatever you buy is fine.' The tears ran down her mother's cheeks and, taking out all her money, she bought her daughter a dress made of heavy crimson silk. Suisui put it on, then plaited her hair in a thick braid behind her head. Her mother led her forward a few steps, then stopped her and stepped back to admire her. She was startled to realize that her girl was a real beauty. If only… if only her eyes were as bright as they had once been, she would be a goddess.

Unbeknownst to Suisui's mother, at that very moment, the director of the All-China New Year's TV Show, the mustachioed and gimlet-eyed Mr Zhang Shan, was looking at the tapes of Suisui. He ran them through several times then issued his order: 'Put her on last! If you put her on first, no one will watch the rest of the programme.' The executive director, Tian Li, was almost lost for words. 'Are you telling me, put her top of the bill?' 'Of course! She's superb, the real thing! Can't you see?' 'But isn't she a bit wet behind the ears?' protested Tian Li. 'I'll tell you who's wet behind the ears!' roared his boss. 'Those pop stars we have to put on, they can't sing to save their lives. They don't take anyone in with their tricks. The girl has a celestial voice. The viewers can tell quality when they see it, you just watch the reaction she gets!'

Suisui caused a sensation among the cast when she was recording. They all wanted to watch this young blind woman sing her flower songs. Suisui tried to imagine what they were like from the sound of their voices. One, in particular, struck her forcefully, a pleasant male baritone that sounded something like the wind on Pine Crag, and something like the water in the healing springs, easy and friendly. He introduced himself as Tian Li, the programme producer.

Suisui was fascinated by his voice. He reminded her of her young singing partner at the songfest. Too bad he missed out on being Emperor of Flower Songs; she had been crowned Empress that day instead. The crown had been woven of grass and wild peonies and, although she could not see it, she had smelled its sweet perfume and had sensed the ephemeral delicacy of the fresh flowers.

If Suisui had been able to see, her eyes would have shown her a tall young man who towered over her diminutive frame. Tian Li could see her, however, and he very much liked what he saw. He found himself thinking, *If only this lass wasn't blind…*

The New Year's Eve Show that year was a great success, Suisui's singing brought the house down, and before the show was finished, the phones were ringing off the hook. The presenter had the bright idea of telling callers: 'We're delighted that our Empress of Flower Songs won your hearts, but, you know what? She's blind, and has been since a high fever robbed her of her sight when she was eight. All you lovely people who enjoyed her singing so much, please see if you can think of a way to restore her sight. We would so love young Suisui to be able to see again!' The presenter's rousing speech went out live across the nation. Listeners were moved to tears, and racked their brains to find some way to help.

Tian Li was one of them. After the Chinese New Year, he had two projects: to seek medical treatment for Suisui's sight; and to set up a solo concert for her. Hong Kong and Taiwan singers had once been all the rage but nowadays their coquettish affectations and woeful lyrics no longer appealed the way they used to. A new face was needed, a new style, new songs! And Suisui seemed to have come on the scene at just the right moment. The question was, how to package her, how to position her? She was a lovely girl, with a voice of pure gold, but she still had to be presented just right. If you got her image just slightly wrong, there would be no correcting it.

Tian Li had started off as a designer and had a particular interest in creating someone's image. He dashed off dozens of sketches of Suisui, and settled on one showing her dressed in a red top and green trousers, with her hair caught up on top with a comb. That was, he felt, something completely fresh and new for a singer, and just right for an Empress of Flower Songs. Just as he was putting the finishing touches to his artwork, the phone rang and he was summoned to the departmental office for a meeting with Zhang Shan, who had recently been promoted to director. He thought he might as well take his sketches along with him.

Zhang Shan lowered his voice conspiratorially: 'Do you remember that before the Cultural Revolution there was a songwriter called Wu Miao?' he asked Tian Li. Startled, Tian Li burst out: 'Why yes! My dad used to say she was the greatest! Then she mysteriously disappeared…' 'Well, now she's reappeared.' Zhang Shan fingered his moustache and gave Tian Li a sidelong glance. 'And guess who she is? Suisui's mother!'

Tian Li cracked his finger joints and said nothing for a moment. Suisui's mother – that plump, sloppily-dressed middle-aged woman of no apparent significance. It seemed ludicrous to link her with the once glorious Wu Miao.

'Are you sure?'

'Quite sure.' Zhang Shan flicked through the sketches Tian Li had brought with him and picked the one of Suisui in a red top and green trousers: 'This one's good, but it still needs a tweak. Give her a flower crown on her head and a garland on her neck, and flare the trouser legs and sleeves. That way, you're creating something new out of a traditional look. What do you think?'

Tian Li thought it sounded more like the get-up of a Hawaiian hula dancer. But he said nothing. He was just grateful that the director was thinking more or less along the same lines as he was.

Tian Li went to see Suisui. He had ten of his costume designs made up, took them with him and made her try them on. The red top and green trouser look did not look quite right.

What Suisui actually wore that day was a white outfit, the top embroidered with silver peonies and a crimson silk sash tied twice around her waist, making her look hour-glass slender. She really did have a flower crown on her head, made of wild flowers, and when she was led onto the stage by the presenter, there were gasps from the audience, and a sigh of relief from Tian Li backstage; her image had struck the right note.

Suisui's first flower song was the one she sang so often, 'Twelve Months of Love':

...The seventh month comes and we sun-dry the wheat
The orioles we reared are sold,
Never mind how much we earned
What counts is that you love me...

The eighth month, the fifteenth day, in the moonlight
This fresh fruit is priceless
Have you the desire to swallow it down?
This lass silently offers it to you.

The ninth month comes, and nine great suns
And yellow chrysanthemums shine golden, oh!
When she thinks how handsome you are
This lass's heart is fit to break.

The tenth month comes and the wheat's been threshed
The ox drags the grinding stone round and round
If you're dead, I'll follow you to the grave
If you're alive, I'll be here waiting oh!

The eleventh month comes and the crags are cold
Under the ice bridge, piles of hemp seed paste
I fall on the kang and weep for three days oh!
Our little home's like an icehouse.

The last month of the year, on the eighth day
The ice freezes three feet thick
I cannot eat, I cling to the walls
My body is sick with love of you.

As Suisui finished 'Twelve Months of Love', there was a burst of applause. She went on to sing 'Three Peaks of Hezhou', 'Dried Flowers', 'Anna's Garland of Flowers', and 'Sing La La'. And when she had finished all the songs she had prepared, she sang five more. Her mother, concealed backstage, began to worry that if she carried on singing, she'd soon get through all her new material. But then Suisui's solo performance came to an end amid a storm of applause and her mother joined her on stage for five curtain calls. The presenter announced that the songs had all been written especially by Suisui's mother, the celebrated song-writer comrade Wu Miao. Wu Miao, she went on, had been sent down to Hexi along with other city youth during the Cultural Revolution and had stayed on afterwards, spending nearly thirty years studying Hezhou flower songs and making new contributions to this ancient art form. More applause, this time for Wu Miao. The whole of the media pulled out all the stops for this magical mother and daughter pair.

Tian Li got Suisui a large bouquet of pink carnations after that performance. When he went backstage to present them to her, she had pulled off her white silk tunic and was standing in a red silk dudou bodice, beneath which a pair of pert breasts strained at the material like little mushrooms. Tian Li's heart pounded and he hurriedly put the flowers down and left. When her mother came in and said: 'These must be from Mr Tian!' Suisui was appalled. *I was getting changed!* She thought and flushed scarlet. Fortunately, the arrival of more and more bouquets soon distracted her. A sea of flowers filled the little dressing room, and she soon put her embarrassment behind her.

However, the director, Zhang Shan, called Tian Li into his office. Looking anxious, he said:

'Did you sense a problem with Suisui's performance?'

'No!' Tian Li was startled. 'She went down well with everyone. What do you mean?'

There was a long silence, then Zhang handed Tian Li a cigarette and lit one for himself.

'Those flower songs that Suisui's singing, they're not the originals. They're full of grace notes and suchlike, technically much more difficult to sing, but is that interesting? If she carries on like this, she won't be the Empress of Flower Songs anymore.'

Tian Li exhaled:

'Is it that serious?'

'We can't tell that right now, of course, but as all chess-players know, when you make one move, you've got to look three moves ahead. It's her mother Wu Miao I'm worried about, she needs watching… I've been looking into her past, she started out as a singer, and was something of a prodigy, but then for some reason her voice went and she turned to composing. She's definitely the tiger mother type, which of course is quite understandable, but somehow I feel she's a bit over the top.'

Zhang Shan puffed hard on his cigarette.

'I'd love to be wrong.'

Tian Li was silent. He finished his own cigarette and left. He had known Zhang Shan for more than a dozen years and he knew his reputation for being sharp-eyed was fully justified.

Outside, under the stars, Tian Li suddenly felt desolate. Then, as if prompted by some supernatural impulse, he got on his bike, peddled over to the hotel behind the TV station, and went to room 501, where the singer and her mother were staying.

Suisui and her mother gave him a warm welcome. Wu Miao ordered some snacks from room service – sweet glutinous rice balls and Sichuan-style wonton, both of which were very good. When she arrived in Beijing, Wu Miao had gone to a beauty salon for semi-permanent eyebrows and eyeliner, but, in Tian Li's view, such over-liberal eye-makeup on an older woman only made her look older. Now she asked him to take the sofa, while she and Suisui sat cross-legged on the carpet, as a mark of respect. The snacks arrived and Wu Miao stirred them with the spoon and blew on the bowls, in case he should burn his tongue, after which she almost spoon-fed him.

'Mr Tian,' she began. 'What do you think about Suisui. Should I take her to get the same done to her eyebrows and eyes too? I mean, all the Beijing girls do, and I think she could do with some plastic surgery too, like padding out the bridge of her nose. When I mentioned it to her, she acted like I was trying to kill her, but she'd listen to you.'

Tian Li smiled: 'Mrs Wu, I think you should listen to your daughter. She's a beautiful young woman now, in her prime, and if you get her plastic surgery, it might ruin her face.'

Wu Miao looked displeased but Suisui laughed with unaffected ease. 'Didn't I tell you so? Give it up, Mum.'

But her mother paid no attention. 'Mr Tian, tell me now, why do you always want Suisui looking so natural? Singers nowadays have to be fashionable, right? Suisui is beautiful of course, but even jade is enhanced with polishing. Plastic surgery would make her even more beautiful, wouldn't it? I'm not going to beat about the bush, after this evening's performance, which she did so well in, we've had a stack of invitations for Suisui to do singing engagements, look!' And she flicked through the invitations. 'We're talking big tycoons here, they're just itching to throw their money around, and Suisui's going to make a big name for herself. She's just got to have the right image!'

Tian Li was not too happy at all this but felt obliged to respond positively. Wu Miao was delighted, and went to fetch a contract out of a small safe.

'Look at this, a Mr Guo sent his manager over with it! He's a big tycoon, and the first thing he said was he'd pay Suisui 5,000 for an appearance. That's not a cent less than Mao Ahmin gets!'

As she spoke the doorbell rang. Wu Miao opened up and beamed a smile: 'We were just talking about you! Let me introduce you: Mr Tian Li, executive director of the New Year's Eve Gala, and Tian Li, this is Mr Guo, the tycoon I was talking to you about.'

Tian Li took a good look. Mr Guo had hatchet features and an intimidatingly bushy pair of eyebrows, but he had a pleasantly deep voice, rare among Beijingers, the sort of voice that could belt out Old Man River and The Volga Boat Song, Tian Li felt.

After exchanging pleasantries, they got down to business. Tian Li already knew that Guo was a showbiz promoter, and wanted to take Suisui on tour. Tian Li was surprised at Wu Miao. She may have had a glorious youth but she had after all been stuck in a remote backwater for years, and he expected she would be fazed by the sudden limelight. But she was absolutely on the ball, very sophisticated. It would be easy enough to let her completely bamboozle you.

Actually, the one who was really bamboozled was Suisui. She heard everyone talking but had not the faintest idea what they were saying. She strained her ears to pick out one voice, the one that was dearest to her. Ever since she had left Pine Crag to come to Beijing, it was this voice that was always there in her hour of need, this voice that made her go red to the ears when she heard it, this voice that made her daydream. She imagined the owner of the voice as a handsome young man, even younger and more handsome than her partner in the Flower Songfest. She thought of him day and night, and felt she was singing her songs just for him, which made them especially moving. She was nineteen but this was the first time she had fallen for a boy, and she was smitten. The rest of the world seemed oh so far away, and she imagined herself as the goddess emerging from the peonies around the Pine Crag springs. Song after song bubbled up inside her.

Inside the moonlight there stands a tree, oh,
And where the tree is, someone is sitting

In the moonlight, a flowering reevesia tree
And under it sits a beautiful girl, oh.

The phoenix spreads its wings and soars 8,000 li
Alights far beyond the Great Wall
Without wings I cannot return home
In my dreams, I look to see if you have come.

The horse between the shafts is beaten with a stick
The whip in the driver's hand is smooth and straight
Seventeen or eighteen young peonies
Have lost their hearts to the youth on his journey.

Red birds hopping, sipping water
Blue birds roosting in the plum tree
The one who leads my heart is you, oh
But who is it that leads your heart?

Wild peonies in the third month are blooming so bonny
The spring waters are so blue it breaks my heart
With every passing day I think of you
I cannot bear to see you go.
....

As Suisui was indulging in these flights of fancy, she heard Tian Li ask: 'Mr Guo, I've been listening to your voice, did you sing yourself when you were young?' Then she heard a laugh: 'People often ask me that. I know I've got a big voice but, sadly, I was always off-key and I never passed the singing exams.' She heard her mother and Tian Li laugh in response, and laughed along with them, a long loud laugh. 'Silly girl, you'll ruin your voice laughing so hard,' her mother chided her. 'Stop laughing! You think you're so grown-up! Far from it! What do you know about scales…do, re, mi, so, la? Have you any idea how many kinds of flower songs there are? All you can do is sing Hezhou songs, you've never even heard of all the other kinds! From now on, you perform at night, and you study flower song music theory all day, no more wasting time!' Her outburst silenced the two men. They had to admire her spirit, but Tian Li felt suddenly exhausted.

This particular tour never went ahead because an invitation to America arrived. Fired up with adrenalin, Wu Miao rushed hither and thither morning, noon and night while Suisui appeared to have nothing to do. She just sat around, smiling vacantly. The costumes she wore for her performances were either chosen by her mother or were personally designed for her by Tian Li, but of that she knew nothing at all.

Four folk singers went on the trip to America, of whom Suisui was the only one singing flower songs. They performed in Washington DC's largest concert hall, and the Secretary of State put in a personal appearance. Suisui's songs were the finale. It was the first time the American audience had heard flower songs, and they were dumbstruck.

Almond blossom time, the second month
Bandits burst into our homestead
They destroyed three thousand books
And burnt the house to the ground.

It was almond blossom time, the second month
The young man wiped his tears dry
He had hidden the Collected Flower Songs in the pickle jar
The pickles were kohlrabi.

The American audience gazed enraptured at the small figure of the Chinese girl on stage, with her unusual tonal quality, the notes drawn out long like the string of a kite, swooping and soaring, hovering endlessly in a cloudless blue sky, making her listeners feel cleansed from the inside out. You could have heard a pin drop after her song drew to a close. To Suisui's mother it felt like an age, though it was probably only a minute, and then there was a thunderous roar. It took Wu Miao a moment to realize that it was a storm of applause and cheers, followed by coloured confetti raining down.

Suisui took nine curtain calls and her mother wept tears of joy. Even Tian Li's eyes were wet.

Overnight, Suisui shot to stardom. Her picture appeared in all the important media. Her strange-sounding songs appealed to American listeners avid for novelty. Of course these listeners had no idea that the songs bore no relation to the authentic flower songs, having been re-packaged by their composers. What held them in awe was Suisui's silvery voice, so different from the coloratura of the sopranos they were accustomed to. Suisui was a natural singer. There was no artifice in her voice – it rang true in the ears of tens of thousands of listeners, something that was not only uncommon, it was almost unimaginable.

But that night did not bring Suisui happiness. It brought her suffering; indeed, it broke her heart.

It was late. Suisui changed back into her normal clothes and Tian Li took her out for a snack as usual. Her mother normally went with her but she was emotionally shattered and wanted some peace and quiet, so she went back to her room. Tian Li took Suisui to a Chinese restaurant, whose owner happened to have been at the performance. He was delighted to have her as a customer, and said the meal was on the house. He also served them some special dishes, like freshwater snails. Tian Li carefully extracted them from their shells, took one between his chopsticks and fed it to Suisui. 'Good?' he asked.

Suisui nodded and smiled, and then the tears came. Tian Li was horrified. What was up with Suisui this evening?

They had spent nearly a year together by then. Suisui was a quiet girl, not much of a talker, who preferred smiling her quiet, uncomplicated smiles. He often asked her: 'Do you have any vision at all, even vaguely?' But the answer was always no, nothing. Tian Li simply could not imagine what it felt like for a beautiful young woman to be totally blind. More than that, for a world of bright colours to have disappeared overnight and turned into impenetrable darkness. She inspired great tenderness in Tian Li, and not only tenderness.

Tian Li was not yet thirty but had been in the entertainment business for a good number of years. Everyone who had been around actors knew they talked and joked non-stop about sex; and almost all the shows full of sexual innuendo that were popular nationwide came from Beijing. Tian Li was a man of the world. Yet faced with Suisui, he felt like he was meeting someone from another planet, she was so extraordinary. Girls of her age in Beijing were all sophisticates who were anything but innocent, whatever they might claim. By comparison, Suisui was like a fallen star, so bright, pure and beautiful that he could scarcely believe it. She was made of crystal. Her fragility terrified him. He may have been a seasoned campaigner but he had no idea how to make a move on her. The first time the urge came to him, he found himself strongly drawn towards her, and just as strongly repelled. He was flummoxed.

Of course he wanted her, that was normal for a healthy young man like himself. She had haunted his dreams ever since that day that he had seen her in the changing room. But he also knew that he could say nothing or he would frighten her off and ruin their friendship.

He never in a million years imagined that it was she who would come on to him.

'Mr Tian, why are you so good to me?' she said now.

He flushed. 'Why shouldn't I be? Everyone wants to be good to you, if I can serve you in anything then it's my pleasure.'

Suisui's tears continued to fall. 'Mr Tian, you're teasing me, just talking nonsense, I know what you're doing! I just want to ask you one question, please give me an honest answer. Do you pity me because I'm blind?'

If only Suisui could have seen him. Tian Li went as red as a ripe tomato and began to tremble. He suddenly felt that this girl, completely unaffected by city life, was not blind at all but was using her eyes to see into the innermost parts of his being.

His voice shaking, he said: 'What are you saying? You're an amazing woman, I've never thought of you as blind.'

Suisui stretched out a hand and tearfully patted his neck: 'You're so wonderful, that was just what I wanted to hear! I'm nineteen, and I know that makes me young in city terms, but it's not young where I come from. I've grown up fatherless and my mum's brought me up well but she scares me, and I can't talk to her about what I feel. Ever since I went blind, I've felt wretched, but even though I can't see you, as soon as I heard your voice, I knew what I wanted…I…I'm telling you, every time I sing, I tell myself that I'm singing for you and that makes me sing well. Really! Do you believe me?'

Tian Li felt something wet and icy cold running down his cheeks. Tears? He could hardly believe it. It had been many, many years since someone had made such a heartfelt declaration to him. He had lived a lie, year after year, and for an instant, hearing the truth felt quite unbearable. But after all, he was a man who saw life through the prism of the hardships he had undergone. True, he wasn't expecting this and he felt quite emotional, but not for long. He quickly pulled himself together and began to apply a cool head to the situation: he had to think of a response that neither echoed her nor hurt her.

'Suisui,' he began, lighting a cigarette and taking a puff, to calm his beating heart. 'Thank you. Thank you for the trust you have in me. I really value the genuineness of your feelings, but you're at the peak of a brilliant career. You should be devoting yourself to it heart and soul, not getting distracted by things that have nothing to do with your singing. When you stop singing, then we'll see…'

'What's singing?' Suisui protested, 'you know that we call Pine Crag "Song Mountain"? Everyone there can sing flower songs. We just sing what we feel like, what's the big deal? Singing can never be nearly as big as my feelings, don't you see?…Tian Li, I've wanted someone to love me all my life. I've heard the story in the song the goddess handed down to us. I wanted to be that goddess myself, beloved by the huntsman. After I went blind, I thought that if only someone would love me for myself, then I might recover my sight. Tian Li, what are you doing? You're not laughing at me, are you?'

Tian Li sighed a deep sigh. How could he not find Suisui attractive? Any man would, she was adorable. But they did not live in a romantic age like in the olden days, this was the age of realism. Never mind that Suisui was blind, he would never dare get involved with a girl like her. She was too pure and too unworldly; she would throw herself in at the deep end, give her all to him. You might expect to find someone like her as the aesthetic character in a novel, but if you met one in real life, the only thing to do was to turn tail and run, because if you weren't careful you would bring down on yourself some mad passion which could prove fatal. At twenty-nine, Tian Li had been through the mill with his love life, and he was just an ordinary bloke, with no desire to play the classic romantic lead. He was perfectly satisfied with his life as it was; it was pleasant and uncomplicated. One day he would settle down and find himself a suitable wife. It was either screw around first and then stick with one wife, or marry too soon and end up screwing around afterwards.

But how could he explain himself to this girl who was as crystal clear as water. He puffed away at his cigarette, finally stubbing it out fiercely in the ashtray, saying: 'It's getting late, Suisui, we'd better go.'

The owner reiterated that their dinner was on the house, asking only that Suisui sign the visitors' book with its yellow brocade cover, and then personally escorted them to the door. Embarrassed at his generosity, Suisui insisted on giving him the red sash in which she had performed, for which he thanked her profusely.

Tian Li and Suisui walked away without speaking. When they got to the corner, Suisui missed her step and almost fell, and Tian Li grabbed hold of her. He felt again how delicate she was, and at the same moment, Suisui felt the strength of the arm that was holding her up. Emboldened by the darkness, they simultaneously turned to each other and embraced.

It was the first time in Suisui's young life that she had felt such overpowering emotion, and almost overcome by ecstasy she trembled from head to foot. Her face was beaded with moisture, tears or sweat, she did not know, she could only keep repeating: 'Oh, Tian Li, Tian Li, you good man!' Tian Li was conscious only of her breath, which had a musky sweetness, like fresh orchids. The night sky was clear, too wonderful for words, and he seemed to be caught up in a fairy tale, with a fairy in his arms. For a flesh and blood man like him, in such a situation, even if the Buddha himself had appeared before him, he could not have controlled his impulses.

That night, Suisui lay awake. She was aware of her mother quietly opening the door to see if she was asleep; and then Tian Li doing the same. After Tian Li delivered her to the hotel, he had not left. Her mother had helped get her ready for bed. Tian Li would surely want to talk to her about Suisui and himself. At the thought, her heart pounded and she knew without seeing that her face was aflame. But she was happy too and, as she listened to her heart beating hard, she said to herself, *Tian Li, tell her, I'm not afraid!*

Eventually she could not contain herself any longer and crept out of her room, soundlessly, so familiar was she with her surroundings.

When the second door she passed through banged, she thought her heart would stop, but no one stirred. As her heart resumed its normal rhythm, an odd thing happened: she seemed to see the colours of the rainbow flashing before her, then vanishing instantaneously. She was excited. *The goddess is speaking to me*, she thought. *My eyes are going to get better, my sufferings will be over....*

But just then fragments of conversation coming from her mother's room ended her happiness once and for all.

'...Mr Tian, Suisui's eyes will never get better, let it go....'

'No, I owe Suisui, I owe her a lot... I won't be able to bear it if I can't do anything to help her...'

'...Don't say that, I know we can't possibly presume to get her special treatment, that's just who she is, that's not your fault, it's my stupid fault. If you really want to help her, get her some TV appearances, TV's where it's at, that's where to get your face known, and looked after too, and Suisui's such a bright girl...'

'Of course I can do that, no problem. But I have the feeling that's not what Suisui really wants.'

'What do you mean?'

'Obviously... she really wants to get her sight back.'

'Ah-ya! Don't keep going on about that, Mr Tian! How can I make you understand? Let me spell it out tonight, once and for all. That's not going to happen, you know that, I know that, and God knows it too! I don't want you bringing it up again tomorrow!'

Suisui stood rooted to the spot, for an instant that seemed to last a thousand years. The two in the bedroom caught the faintest sound of a sigh, instantly swallowed up in the utter silence.

Suisui's mother poured Tian Li a glass of wine, and filled her own glass too: 'People of our age should drink slowly, it's foreign wine, we're not used to it, but it's not bad stuff, better than nothing...You know who I am, Tian Li. I can be a bit prickly, I've seen too much of the world. I've had my fair share of suffering, almost died, nothing scares me! I talk weird don't I? I've spent thirty years in the North-West, so naturally I picked up the dialect, but no way am I a hick from the sticks! I'm Wu Miao! You have heard of me, haven't you? I was a hit singer and composer in the 1960s, back then there weren't many people like me who could do both! You never heard of me? That's because of your age, you were only just born in the 60s. Cheers…!'

Tian Li stared at the woman in front of him, at her face raddled with age and all that she had been through. As she spoke of time passing, the years seemed to drop from her, and he could well imagine the wrinkles vanishing and the good looks she must once have had. She must have been a real beauty.

'You know the saying that beautiful women come to a bad end… it's no word of a lie.' Wu Miao gulped the wine as if she was drinking water. 'If you don't stick up for yourself, people do you down. If you do stick up for yourself, you get their backs up – people are so resentful. No one ever comes to help in your hour of need! Just when I was most popular, I got into trouble, because I said a Soviet artiste wasn't very good, and that made me a "Rightist". I was furious. I was an impetuous young woman, the stress broke my health, and damaged my vocal chords too. In those days, I had no money, so I just had to get on with life as best I could. Then I met Suisui's father, the coward, it wasn't outsiders who kicked up a fuss, it was him…but enough of that…'

Tian Li watched in astonishment as she took another large swig. He felt like reminding her that this was foreign wine and she really shouldn't drink it as if it were her North-Western hot sweet potato wine.

'The only thing I've wanted all my life is for Suisui to carry on where I left off, and not have to suffer the way I did!' said Wu Miao, and a tear forced its way from the corner of each dried-up eye socket.

'Everything I've done, it's been for her… You think she really lost her sight when she got a high fever? Oh, no, it wasn't that at all!'

Their voices sank lower, but Wu Miao's whisper was amplified in the stillness of the night. Then came the fateful words: 'I blinded her with the waters of the healing spring, that's what I did!'

She had scarcely finished speaking when there was the faintest sound outside, but it instantly vanished.

Tian Li sprang to his feet in shock. The woman in the dim lamplight of the room seemed suddenly utterly malevolent:

'How… how could you have done something like that?'

'I…I did it for her own good! That child is such a talented singer but she lets her heart run away with her. I was afraid that she'd fall in love when she got a bit older and her character would change, and I'd never make a singer of her. There was that time when she missed her audition and I was so furious! But I sorted her out, and made sure she focused completely on her singing, on the flower songs, and she was crowned Empress and her career took off. There's no one in Pine Crag that won't tell you this: it was after she went blind that Suisui became a fine flower song singer!'

Tian Li was lost for words. He had no idea that mothers like this existed. The woman must be mentally ill.

'The world came to an end for me that day, it was like I died …' The tears were flowing more freely now. 'I gave Suisui three sleeping pills and made sure she was sleeping soundly, then I heated some water, and sponged her down. Then, I'd heard the old folks say that if you heated the spring water in the medicine pot, the steam was extremely toxic…I don't regret it, no I don't, everyone says that Suisui only became a fine singer after she went blind!'

There was a bang outside, as if something had been overturned. This time both of them heard it and, startled, rushed out of the room. Nothing. The wind must have blown the potted plants off the window ledge outside the shuttered windows.

That evening, Suisui's mother got very drunk, and did not wake until noon the next day. She had a terrible headache, it felt as if needles were being drilled into her skull. The door to the adjoining room was ajar and she looked in: the quilt had not been folded and there was no one there. She imagined that Tian Li had come to take Suisui out for a walk, as he'd been doing every morning lately. There was a small wood nearby, which was nicely kept and very pretty.

She endured her pounding headache and made a good meal, intending for it to serve as lunch and dinner combined, giving Suisui time to get ready – she had an evening performance that day.

But she waited until evening and still no one came.

As the evening mist drew in, Tian Li turned up. Wu Miao's heart began to drum in her chest. In unison, they asked each other: 'Where's Suisui?'

They both knew this was not good. Wu Miao put on her outside shoes, her hands trembling so much she could not tie the laces, but she still insisted: 'Nothing's wrong, it can't be. She's blind, how far can she have got on her own?' They split up and searched until nightfall. Then Tian Li suddenly realized he should have contacted the American promoters, to discuss changing the order of the programme. If Suisui was really lost, they would have to change the programme, wouldn't they? Phone, he needed a phone; he'd tell them Suisui had fallen ill… On his way back to the hotel, he saw Wu Miao ahead of him. The way she was walking, she looked like an old woman. That gave him a bad fright. How could someone get so old so quickly?

They walked into the hotel, and what they saw startled them out of their wits. In the cavernous dining room, there sat Suisui, all on her own, eating her dinner. At a second glance, they saw her face was reddened and puffed up, but her expression was as calm as they had ever seen it. It was as if she had grown up overnight. But most alarming was the way she was eating: the table was covered with dishes of food, which she was ploughing her way through doggedly. She looked prepared to devour an entire haunch of venison.

'Suisui!' Wu Miao called tentatively.

Suisui did not respond, just carried on with her meal, her cheeks bloated with food. Wu Miao and Tian Li stood rooted to the spot until finally Wu Miao took fright and went and threw arms around her daughter: 'Suisui, what's all this about?! Stop eating! You'll make yourself ill! You haven't forgotten you've got a performance tonight?'

'Of course, I haven't forgotten, how could I?' Suisui sounded calm.

For Tian Li, it was this very calmness that filled him with foreboding.

Soon enough, Suisui got them to lead her to her dressing room, so the makeup artist could do her makeup. As Tian Li helped her up the stairs he could not help but be astonished at the difference between yesterday and today: then, this girl had felt as fluid as water, today she was hardened, physically close to him, yet somehow in a different universe. Unlike her normal self, she fussed over her makeup, complaining at every stroke of the powder brush on her face, rubbing it off and re-applying it, spending half-an-hour on drawing one eyebrow. Finally the makeup artist lost patience: 'Now then, Miss, you're pretty enough.'

'But I can't see it,' said Suisui.

'Then ask this gentleman.'

'Mr Tian, look at me, am I pretty?'

When Tian Li thought back on it, these were the last words Suisui ever spoke to him. He found his voice shaking a little as he answered: 'Yes, you're beautiful.'

Suisui's mouth widened in a smile, an odd smile: the corners twitched, flecks of face powder dropped off, and Tian Li realized that overnight, the shape of her face had changed. It seemed to be covered with a rubber mask. The skin had a sinister paleness, and all its former delicacy was gone. Tian Li was alarmed, but dared not say anything when she was about to go on stage. He would have a good talk to her when the performance was over. She must have heard his conversation with her mother the night before; she must have.

Suisui went on stage amid tumultuous applause from the audience. Wu Miao's expression relaxed, but Tian Li was still gripped with anxiety. Suisui was not smiling as they cheered her. Her white outfit no longer made her look like a goddess, but more like a ghost, like Dou E and Li Niang. What inexorable force could have changed an unaffected and guileless girl out of all recognition between one day and the next?

Suisui's opening notes brought Tian Li's heart into his mouth. Her sweet voice had become coarse and harsh; she was howling the words. The American audience, however, loved it and there was a storm of applause.

> *I have tumbled into sleep*
> *A creature of evil*
> *I sicken for my beloved*
> *He is covered in mutton fat*
> *I cannot tell why*
> *Mother has a bad conscience*

Tian Li and Wu Miao exchanged glances. There was fear in their looks: this was like no flower song they had ever heard. It was utterly desolate, like a reproach from the very earth itself. Tian Li felt his heart beating faster, and he saw Suisui's mother begin to tremble.

> *I changed my coarse sackcloth*
> *All for you*

The fragrant flowers wrapped in the hand towel
Gaze into this lass's blind eyes
My tears fall
I am living in anguish.

Can you hear how this lass's voice has changed?
Oh unfortunate girl
She is an American candle weeping tears of wax
There is no greater pain and misery in this world
A whole generation
The hearts and thoughts of the living are destroyed

My God, thought Tian Li, finding the words and Suisui's sorrowful tone unbearably sad. No matter what, as soon as the performance was over, he would go and tell Suisui that he loved her, just the same way as she loved him, and if she could wait a few more years until she was a little older, he would marry her. He would never find another woman like her in his life, and if he did not tell her what was in his heart, what kind of a man was he?

But just as these thoughts were going through his mind, Suisui's voice cracked and tore like rending silk, one long-drawn-out note soaring into the air, then suddenly snapping off.

A deathly silence fell in the auditorium. Tian Li saw Wu Miao go waxy pale and then faint. There was uproar.

Tian Li did not know how much time had passed but he was finally able to pull himself together. He burst into the artists' dressing room, but the huge space seemed to have been divided up into countless small squares. It felt like a maze. He ran from square to square, and each square held a woman sitting in front of a mirror but none of them was Suisui. He must be going mad.

The nation's TV stations broadcast the entire scene, sending chills down viewers' spines. Sitting in his five-star hotel room in Beijing, Mr Guo the tycoon heaved a sigh in that unusual baritone of his and slowly tore Suisui's contract into tiny pieces. As he cast the fragments from the window, they fluttered earthwards and were swallowed up in the infamous Beijing smog.

With the economic reforms of the 1980s and 90s, Pine Crag and its healing springs were developed into a tourist destination. The Pine Crag folk knew they had Suisui to thank for that. She had left Pine Crag, achieved fame in the outside world, and never returned. Yet every evening as they walked back from their fields, they heard her sing her flower songs, her voice wafting down to them from the top of the mountain.

The first month comes and it's Spring, oh!
Red lanterns hang from the farmhouse gate
You can ask up and down the village
They'll all say I don't fancy you.

The second month comes and the dragon looks up, oh!
Third sister Wang will toy with a bridal garland
With no one around, I'll take your hand
If someone comes, you hide back there.

The third month comes, and on the third day, oh!
The Queen Mother of the West has her birthday
Our beloved girl sits on the ground
Singing her youth away.

The fourth month comes and peonies bloom
Little sister's eyes are plucked out
The young man, oh, he goes away
Leaving his lover behind.

The fifth of the fifth, it's the Dragon Boat feast
Let's drink ruby wine, oh!
Let's open King Yama's Roll of the Dead
You and I are fated to stay together

The sixth month comes, oh, and five red waves
I wash my clothes in clear water
I miss you by day, dream of you by night
I cry enough tears to flood a gully

The way the Pine Crag folk tell it, Suisui is the goddess who bequeathed her song to Pine Crag and then left them. But she still misses them and comes back every evening to sing a flower song for villagers returning home from a day of hard toil.

A Classic Tragedy

Xuanming was the seventeenth daughter in a large family. One of her prized possessions was a photograph of the Pearl Concubine, a distant relative of hers, she said. The Pearl Concubine was nothing like as beautiful as legend had it, being fat, with somewhat expressionless eyes, but she enjoyed a high reputation amongst our people, possibly because of the unusual manner of her death. (People tend to love and cherish the dead more than they do the living. If the dead had souls, they would no doubt regret dying, and even if they were able to take human form again, they would still find themselves enmeshed in life's hardships.)

Xuanming, on the other hand, was a real beauty. One autumn day, Aunt Jade, a relative on her mother's side, arrived at the house. Xuanming was a young girl who had seen a lot of the world because of the kind of family she lived in, but she had never seen anyone as beautiful as Aunt Jade, even in paintings or plays. Aunt Jade had a melancholy beauty, with luminous skin, fine features and a bright red birthmark between her eyebrows. Xuanming's mother, Lady Yang, told her that her Aunt Jade's looks should have made her an imperial concubine and yet she had never married, instead spending all day indoors busy at her needlework, unseen by any man. Every piece of her embroidery was good enough to be sent to the palace but Aunt Jade was adamant that nothing could be sold, or given as a palace gift, until after her death. She bequeathed these assets to Xuanming's family in gratitude for their kindness to her during her life. Lady Yang wept as she told her daughter the story.

'The Lady Concubine showed me endless favour, and now I want you to use all this to buy a dowry with it, for Xuanming,' said Aunt Jade calmly.

Back then, Aunt Jade often took Xuanming into the garden in the early morning before the dew was gone, to pick armfuls of flowers – rose balsam, jasmine and pinks… Then she would have Xuanming carefully pull open the blossoms and pick out the stamens, which she pounded to a paste to make rouge. Aunt Jade's rouge was smooth and fine, a lovely colour, and all the women of the family wanted to use it.

Aunt Jade was a mere twenty-six years old when she fell ill with tuberculosis. 'What none of you understand,' said Lady Yang, 'is that she put too much of herself into everything. No wonder she's fallen ill. We can take care of her, of course, but I'm afraid this illness of hers is serious.'

Xuanming spent her days waiting on Aunt Jade in her rooms. Xuanming was one of those girls who reveled in the company of her close friends. She sometimes put on airs with people she didn't know but when she was with someone she really liked and respected, she would pull out all the stops. She would do anything for her mysterious Aunt Jade. Mysterious to Xuanming, that is, because she had no clue as to Aunt Jade's antecedents. Where had she come from? Why was she not married? Why was she so melancholic?

Xuanming naturally wanted to cheer Aunt Jade up, but she had no success at all. One day, having counted the hour on her fingers and deciding it was time for Aunt Jade to get up, she took her a dish of sweetmeats decorated in two different colours. But when she got to her room, she found the mauve, cloud-embroidered bed curtains firmly drawn. It was only after ascertaining that Xuanming was alone that Aunt Jade allowed her in.

When she slipped through the curtains, Xuanming was startled to see Aunt Jade attired in a white silk mourning dress, assembling the pieces of a violet-coloured lamp. Nor was she her normal affectionate self. Eventually Aunt Jade greeted her with a desultory: 'Now you're here, sit down. Is it warm outside?' And she ordered her maid Ying'r: 'Hurry up and pour some tea for Miss Seventeenth.' Xuanming at twelve years old was extremely picky about her tea-drinking, insisting on the finest, most exquisite tea utensils, as Aunt Jade was quite well aware, and so she ordered her maid to bring the turquoise and white tea cups that she normally used herself, and the best Biluochun tea. But today Xuanming was in no mood for tea-drinking. She had eyes only for the beautiful lamp her aunt was holding.

There was something unearthly about this extravagantly delicate crystal object, whose manufacture seemed to capture the very essence of nature itself. When taken apart, the pieces were like blossoms raining down in the autumn winds and covering the ground. Xuanming was mute with astonishment.

She was even more astonished when Aunt Jade said gently: 'Little sister, this illness is no small thing and I'm afraid it will carry me away. The only person I will miss is you. There are many things about me that you don't know. I have a complicated past. By the time I was your age, I had learnt to write many characters. I have always wanted to write my life story but now the lamp oil has run dry and there's no hope of that. So today I've chosen a few stories to tell you. Your family are not interested – they won't listen to these stories, and even if they did listen, they would just make fun of them.' She grasped Xuanming's hands. 'Little sister, have you heard of the Long Hairs?'

Startled, Xuanming nodded. Ever since she was a little girl, her mother had scared her and her sisters into obedience by invoking the Long Hairs. All she knew was that they were also called the Taipings, rebels who for many years had been at war with the Manchu Dynasty. No more than that. Aunt Jade smiled.

'And what do you think of this lamp?'

'What do you mean, Auntie? I may be young and ignorant but I've been to the palace a few times, and I swear that this lamp has no equal among the palace lamps. Heaven and earth have nothing to compare with it!'

Her aunt smiled again.

'This lamp came from the palace of the Long Hairs. I spent a whole five years there, and this is my only memento. Now that you and I have become close, I want to entrust a task to you.'

Xuanming, still astonished, could only nod and acquiesce: 'Whatever you say, Aunt Jade.'

Her aunt gave her a long look.

'You must give this lamp to Master Fa Yan of Golden Pavilion Temple on Xitan Mountain. If you do this for me, I will extend my blessings to you from the Underworld, and any mishaps you suffer will be turned to good account.'

And Aunt Jade commenced a story which seemed to go on and on, for as long as it took to assemble the pieces of the lamp that were scattered across the bed like flower petals.

In the fifty-seventh and fifty-eighth year of the 60-year cycle (1853-54), the Taiping leader Hong Xiuquan set up his Heavenly Capital in what is now Nanjing. His palace was filled with thousands of women, most of whom were from South China. Virgin girls were chosen and brought to the palace at age thirteen. Amongst so many thousands of women, none were without blemish, but so long as they had their feminine charms, that was considered enough. There were also one or two favoured male courtiers who made mischief in dark corners of the palace and were much feared. The worst of the flatterers and fawners was a man called Meng, who was the emperor's closest confidant. He used to cast spells on men and women alike, and almost no one escaped the tangled web of his machinations. Among the few who remained immune to his flattery was Zhao Bicheng, nicknamed Goddess of the Needle for her embroidery skills.

When Bicheng entered the palace women's quarters at the age of fourteen, no food and no words passed her lips for the first three days, until she was persuaded to eat by the kindness of the East King and his chief aide, a lady called Fu Shanxiang. In spite of her exalted position, Shanxiang was always protective of the younger girls. She also appreciated those with skills and talents and, having spotted young Bicheng's intelligence and beauty, took an immediate fancy to her. The pair spent much time composing poetic couplets and became firm literary friends.

On the emperor's birthday, Meng came to the Embroidery Hall to say that the emperor had particularly asked the Goddess of the Needle to embroider a yellow dragon robe for him. Since it was usual for the emperor to receive such a gift on every birthday, the request did not arouse Bicheng's suspicions and she dutifully followed him out of the hall. However, he did not lead her to the emperor's quarters, but to a private room belonging to the emperor's younger sister, Hong Xuanjiao.

By this point in the story, Xuanming had guessed that Bicheng was none other than the pure and noble lady she saw before her. Her aunt must have had immense courage, Xuanming thought, and she could not suppress a shiver of fear.

Bicheng had been at the palace for five years by then, and was nineteen years old. For some time now she had been in love. The object of her affections was a young officer under Commander Yang Xiuqing, the East King of the Taipings. It was meant to be, and this was the way it happened: Shanxiang had commissioned her to make a lined gown for him. The young man in question, by the name of Si Chen, she told her, was a high-ranking officer. He had successfully defended key strongholds, fought a succession of battles and exterminated countless Manchu devils. Now he was about to celebrate his twenty-sixth birthday and the East King wanted Bicheng to embroider a design of lions and tigers on the gown for him. Bicheng worked until dawn. When finally she went to bed, in that state between waking and sleeping, she had a dream: a handsome young general appeared, clad in a white gown and riding a fiery steed. He smiled at her but the lions and tigers embroidered on his gown seemed to come alive, roaring mightily. She started awake in fright. Just at that moment, the palace women came to rouse her. A messenger from the East King had come to fetch the robe, and they all bustled around dressing and adorning her, before escorting her to the sedan chair that would take her to him. 'Bicheng's going to receive rewards,' they laughed. 'For the East King to send a sedan chair for an embroideress is a huge honour. It's never happened before. This girl's fallen on her feet. Let's hope some of her good luck rubs off on us!' Even the sedan bearers suppressed smiles at that.

Bicheng always went unadorned but today she applied just a touch of make-up and looked stunning. The East King could not take his eyes off her. His discomfiture did not escape Shanxiang's notice. She smiled.

'Your Majesty,' she reminded him politely, 'Did you not bring Miss Bicheng here to look at her work and reward her?'

The East King pulled himself together and complimented the embroideress: 'Your work is beautiful, your reputation as the Goddess of Embroidery is well-deserved! I shall personally make sure you are richly rewarded, and it is my wish that henceforth, my gowns and those of my subordinates are all personally embroidered by you.'

And at his command, there appeared before Bicheng a bag stuffed full of the finest Hepu pearls, along with dozens of pieces of jade. Bicheng was so startled that she initially tried to refuse the gift, until Shanxiang glided up to her.

'Take them, Bicheng, they are for you to eat. You should do as the Heavenly King does, take two pearls and one piece of jade at breakfast, and you will find that as the years go by, not only will your skin grow brighter but you will also live longer. The pearls should be boiled inside a piece of beancurd for some hours, until they swell to twice or three times their size, and melt in the mouth. The jade pieces should be simmered in a closely-sealed pot with elm root for a day and a night until they too are soft, and then you eat them with a little sugar. Delicious.'

But Bicheng said quietly: 'Your humble servant is profoundly grateful to His Majesty, but these are too precious for me, I cannot possibly accept them. I beg His Majesty and Sister Shanxiang to keep them.'

She quietly stepped aside, ignoring the king's obvious displeasure, and then happened to catch a glimpse of a man standing behind the monarch: a tall, slender figure, impossibly handsome and the very man she had seen in her dreams. He was wearing the white robe embroidered by her own hands the previous night, and looking straight at her. She saw admiration, approval and love, and flushed scarlet. Was she mistaken at the meaning in his gaze? But their eyes connected and she was quite unafraid.

The East King had a fiery temper and would normally have reacted in fury and castigated this ignorant slave publicly. But today he was in a benevolent mood, and anxious that his trusted commander should have a good time, so he restrained himself. Privately, though, he cursed Bicheng for being so pretty and yet so stubborn, like a knot in elm wood. Seeing his mood, Shanxiang hurriedly pulled Bicheng into a side corridor, where she could collect her reward in silver coins.

'Young miss, you gave me a terrible fright, you have no idea what a temper he has, and you showed him up in front of everyone! Any other day and he would have had you taken away and put to death. Weren't you frightened? Little sister, we have been friends for a long time, let me give you a word of advice. A straight bowstring can only snap; a bent hook will gather honours. Curb your temper while you live in the palace. If you are too unyielding, you will suffer the consequences.'

Bicheng smiled slightly. 'Ill consequences are just what I'm afraid of. It's so extravagant to eat pearls and jade, and surely such waste will not go unpunished.'

Shanxiang was silent for a moment, then said with great seriousness: 'You're not telling me anything I don't know. The kingdom is on the verge of collapse, and we can do nothing about it! I check the East

King's documents every day and, like every king, he has big ideas. The Taiping Kingdom's silver is draining away fast, and our debts are mounting. On top of that, the princess wants to rebuild her palace. The last time this happened, I made one small objection and His Majesty was furious. He had me put in a cangue in the women's quarters for more than a month. That was when I picked up the bad habit of smoking tobacco…Good sister, listen to me, pull back from the brink, never show your feelings, don't play the hero, because it can only hurt you.'

Bicheng was a very intelligent woman and she knew that her mentor's words came from the heart. But everything had happened so quickly, and she had been so unprepared.......

Now, Meng the courtier took Bicheng into a private room in Princess Hong Xuanjiao's quarters. It was in the middle of universal celebrations over Prince Li Xiucheng's triumphant entry into Suzhou and Hangzhou. Everyone from the queen downwards had gathered in the Great Hall of the imperial apartments in the palace, attired in their best clothes; the six palaces were hung with strings of brightly coloured lanterns, and there were fireworks and dance performances. The female officer Loufei from Yichun prefecture was put in charge. She was a clever woman who had earned the trust and affection of the Heavenly King and was a good organizer, attending to every detail. 'Loyal Prince Li's victory has come just before Your Majesty's birthday, clearly because Heaven rewards the virtuous,' she said. 'Would it not be better for the Heavenly King and the Heavenly Brother to celebrate their separate successes jointly, and make the festivities last for several days all over the Taiping Heavenly Kingdom?' Then she turned to Shanxiang: 'Bicheng is in your charge, make sure that the embroiderer women get down to work and prepare new court dragon robes. They need to be ready for this evening!' Loufei was so enthusiastic that Shanxiang could only nod her agreement.

Meng's infatuation with Bicheng was a matter of long standing. She was the only woman in the entire palace who ignored him utterly, and she was also incomparably beautiful. None of the imperial concubines could hold a candle to her. She had a cool elegance, a noble dignity and her morals were above reproach. Meng was tired of mincing court ladies and their idle chatter; he wanted a change, he wanted Bicheng. But even though he had her trapped, he soon discovered that the lady in question was immune to the spells he tried to cast on her.

He tried using more forceful methods, but to his surprise, this delicate-looking young woman was resolute in her rejection of his advances. When he forced her into a corner, she dodged out of the way, gripped his genitals with one slender hand, and tugged hard. He collapsed to the floor in terrible pain, as this exquisite girl turned and left.

Bicheng flung herself back into the festive throng, furious. The concubines all broke out into a sweat when they saw her. Luckily, the Heavenly King's eye did not fall on her, he was busy admiring an eye-catching throne encrusted in jewels. The courtiers clustered round showering congratulations on him, only Bicheng stood to one side with a face like thunder, saying not a word but shaking her head and sighing.

When Fu Shanxiang, richly attired and made-up for the occasion, had offered her congratulations to the East King, she spotted Bicheng and addressed her quietly: 'You stupid girl, don't put on such a sour face, today of all days!'

Bicheng told her in a whisper what had happened, grinding her teeth in fury and finishing with: 'Meng is the scum of the earth, worse than a pig or a dog!'

Shanxiang was shocked. After a long pause, she said slowly: 'This is not good. Run back to the Embroiderers' Hall and sort yourself out some clothes, then go and hide behind the screen to the Welcoming Joy Garden, quick as you can. I'll send Shun'er to you.'

Bicheng opened her mouth to protest but Shanxiang thrust her away, so hard that Bicheng nearly fell over. The East King saw them and reacted with annoyance: 'This is no time for playing around, mind the Heavenly King doesn't beat you both over the head!'

He had scarcely finished speaking before Bicheng was gone, slipping quietly through the crowds. As she turned to take one last look at Shanxiang, tears welled in her eyes, limpid as just-melted mountain snow. Shanxiang saw her agony of distress and could hardly contain her own tears. She called over the maid servant Shun'er and issued her orders, finishing with: 'Bicheng is one of the finest women in the kingdom, if anything happens to her, I'll hold you responsible, you got that?'

Any other servant would have crumbled at these harsh words, but Shun'er was no ordinary servant girl: not good-looking, but exceptionally resourceful and courageous, Shanxiang's right-hand woman. Shun'er instantly took in the seriousness of the situation and was swiftly gone. She was a practitioner of martial arts, light on her feet, and able to move soundlessly through the darkness. She was the perfect person to send on a night-time mission.

By this time, the Heavenly King had completed his tour of the palace and returned to the jade dais. As the courtiers prostrated themselves in front of him, he sat down on his jewel-encrusted throne, then suddenly guffawed with laughter and addressed his concubines: 'Heaven has bestowed on me ladies of such ineffable intelligence!' And he ordered them to drink up and be merry. Princess Hong Xuanjiao arrived in her phoenix carriage, arrayed in gorgeous clothing, and ordered the concubines to present essays and eulogies to add lustre to the imperial enterprise. 'And where is our son Meng?' she exclaimed. 'When is the Heavenly King to be presented with his new dragon robe? Bring Meng here!'

The three words, 'Bring Meng here!' sounded like a death knell in Fu Shanxiang's heart. She had a terrible feeling that this entire business had been planned. Yet why would the princess choose today to make a scene in front of her brother? She was close to the king, after all. But her train of thought was interrupted by the arrival of Meng himself. He trotted in, bearing in his hands the yellow imperial hat and dragon robe.

The history books have given all sorts of accounts of Shanxiang's sudden disappearance. But Xuanming was sure that the reason was her close relationship to her Aunt Jade. That is to say, the Goddess of the Needle, Zhao Bicheng, as she was then known. There were, however, plentiful accounts of Bicheng in unofficial tales of the Taiping Army, and all agree that she suffered death either by a thousand cuts or by roasting over a slow fire. Even the most sceptical historians are in no doubt that she did die, and her demise is recounted with great relish: Meng the courtier knelt before the king and pulled open the supremely beautiful imperial hat, only to reveal the inside smeared and stained with blood! He set up a wail: 'Your unworthy servant has failed in his duty! Let that brazen hussy Zhao Bicheng find a place to hide herself now! She has polluted this brocade with her filthy woman's secretions, we have clear evidence and testimonies to attest to it. I beg his Majesty to state his desires.'

Shanxiang never forgot how the king's smile froze on his face, which turned the colour of clay. It was a terrifying sight. He seized the brocade hat and inspected it, then flung it to the ground. The courtiers were all rooted to the spot, and certain of the more timid concubines teetered and almost fell. The Heavenly King quickly recovered his composure, and turned a cold gaze on the East King. 'Tell me, East King, how should we proceed?' The latter shot Shanxiang a fierce look: 'According to the dictates of the Heavenly Kingdom, so great a crime calls for the ultimate penalty, a slow roasting in public. This must never happen again.' The Heavenly King concurred: 'We therefore delegate this to the East King. Ensure an interrogation is carried out to find the culprit, then execute them.' He spoke with such cold fury that his courtiers trembled with fear. After a long pause, Shanxiang tried to wipe the sweat from her face, only to find herself too weak to lift her arm. All fell to their knees before the awe-inspiring majesty of the Heavenly King.

On that fear-filled (for Bicheng) night a century ago, brocade-coated guards swiftly surrounded the Embroidery Hall and detained all the embroiderer girls, putting them into the East King's jail. The East King was well aware that the only one missing among his trembling captives was Zhao Bicheng. Shaoxiang was clearly one step ahead of him, he thought.

At that precise moment, Zhao Bicheng was hurrying towards a hamlet a hundred *li* from the capital, dressed as a village woman and armed with a travel permit. She had found the Welcoming Joy Garden in the dark, after which Shun'er had quickly arrived and pushed open the screen to reveal a huge western-style painting. She put her finger on the mouth of one of the cupids and the painting swung back. They stepped into a secret passage, at the end of which was a big door. Rushed though she was, Shun'er did not forget to thrust a bundle into Bicheng's arms.

'This is from Shunxiang,' she said. 'A memento of your long friendship. She says she will be gone one of these days too, and says you should take good care of yourself and find a good man to marry. There's a travel permit inside the bundle. Open it when you get outside. It will let you pass without hindrance anywhere in the Heavenly Kingdom.'

Bicheng wept as she listened to Shun'er, struggling to speak through her tears. 'But what will happen to you and Shunxiang after I've gone?'

Shun'er said nothing, just pushed Bicheng into the passage and hurriedly pulled the painting back into place. She must surely have made up her mind to die.

Three days later, the executioner made his announcement: in the case of the Embroidery Hall, only Zhao Bicheng would be executed. The rest would all be flogged, and the punishments would be carried out at night. The condemned girl was to die by slow roasting – that is, her body was wrapped in cloths steeped in oil, then hung upside down and the feet set alight. When the executioner and his squad arrived, he found Fu Shanxiang in attendance, and the prisoner already bundled in white silk. But when he tried to verify her identity, Shanxiang shouted at him: 'The East King has personally ordered me to supervise the execution, if you mistrust me, you mistrust the king himself.' And the execution squad backed off in alarm.

The execution was carried before the door of the East King's palace, where the prisoner hung suspended from a cassia tree. She burned all through the night. Shanxiang stood at the window, the firelight playing over her expressionless face.

Not long after this, Shanxiang herself disappeared, leaving not a trace behind, vanishing so completely that one might have doubted if she had ever existed.

On that terrible night in Jinling a century ago, the real hero was, I believe, Shun'er. A myriad of tiny clues all point to one conclusion: it was she who died in Bicheng's place. We may imagine the chaos in the East King's palace when Shun'er returned. All the women, including Shanxiang, wanted nothing more than to vanish into the earth, or to slip into a drawer like a piece of folded paper, or to transform into a wisp of cloud, or the wing of a bird, or a drop of water that might turn to steam and evaporate. There was only one exception: Shun'er. That night, as illuminations bright as daylight cast a huge shadow before her, Shun'er had marched straight to the East King's palace, to her certain death.

Of course, she and Shanxiang must have argued fiercely beforehand, but for the first time in her life, Shun'er disobeyed her mistress. She had made her mind up. In her simple heart, she knew that someone had to take Bicheng's place, and if it wasn't her, then it would be someone else. As a mother forgives her child, she forgave the world its iniquities, and walked alone to her death. She was only nineteen when she willingly gave her soul to the darkness of the abyss. She was not a beauty; she was a simple villager from outside Jinling, who had never experienced love. But, unlike the other girls, she had volunteered to enter the Heavenly Palace because she admired the Taiping Uprising. The Taipings had brought her great happiness, albeit for all too brief a time. She had gazed adoringly at the Heavenly King Hong Xiuquan and the East King Yang Xiuqing, though she had never dared to look young commanders like Shi Dakai and Chen Yucheng in the eyes, and blushed involuntarily if she caught sight of them. On many an occasion she had thought that, should there be a need to die, she would do it without complaint, come hell or high water, and there would be no need for anyone to know. But five years of living in the Heavenly Kingdom had turned into a nightmare, and there was not a single night that she had not made the sign of the cross before going to sleep and murmured: 'Oh Lord, forgive them their sins.'

Now she was ready to lay down her life for others. She had not been close to Bicheng, but it was she who had been the go-between, carrying the messages between Bicheng and Shanxiang. Once, Bicheng had been in a very good mood and had presented her with a pair of shoe insoles embroidered by her own hand. Shun'er treasured them, keeping them at the bottom of her trunk. On that last day, she took them out for the first time and put them in her shoes. The colours of the embroidered mandarin ducks were as fresh as ever, embodying Bicheng's wish that she should find love and marriage. But Shun'er could not wait that long.

She repaid this debt of gratitude by dying, hanging herself with a length of white silk. Shanxiang stroked the body, and cried bitterly. She knew that Shun'er had chosen to hang herself instead of using a dagger because that way she would not give Shanxiang the trouble of cleaning up the blood. Now, her erstwhile mistress took her favourite dress, dressed Shun'er's body in it and instructed two of the more reliable maids to wrap her corpse tightly from head to toe in a whole bolt of silk. With the bundle laid out in front of them, Shanxiang led everyone from the women's quarters in prayers.

A heavenly choir was heard, accompanied by a fierce gust of wind. And, in the wind, the women felt someone gazing at them. Someone ensconced within the bosom of the moon. Someone with a gaze that was cool and bright, yet full of longing.

Pompom

On a few windless days in the fifth month of the lunar calendar, Beijing is fleetingly beautiful. The sun dazzles overhead and emerald green foliage burgeons luxuriantly on the trees. But in this city, trees are only clothed in their natural color for a short time, after which every type of particulate matter and dust paints them a uniform grey.

It is on just such a day that Pompom walks through Hezi's door. She is still a tiny puppy, barely weaned, pure white in colour, with eyes that alternate between emerald and aquamarine. She lurches round Hezi and her son, Huanhuan, on ungainly puppyish legs until Hezi, who has no idea what to feed her, cuts up a tiny bit of prawn. Pompom licks the pink meat with her translucent pink tongue, then gobbles it up. Huanhuan offers watermelon, and Pompom eats that too, then boldly gets on her hind legs, puts her front paws on Huanhuan's knee and begs for more.

Hezi has always been afraid of dogs. And not just dogs, but all small creatures. She finds their unsmiling stares rather sinister. It is the opposite with Huanhuan. An only child with few friends, he adores dogs and cats. One day on the way to the supermarket, he becomes instantly smitten with a street merchant's dog and stops, refusing to budge. When his mother drags him away, he keeps looking back.

Finally, he sets up a despairing wail and scalding hot tears drip down his face, wetting his mother's hand. Hezi has been divorced for some time; mother and son only have each other. Faced with Huanhuan's distress, Hezi eventually gives in. From a starting price of 600 yuan, she beats the stallholder down and the puppy is theirs for 220 yuan.

The puppy needs a name. Huanhuan wants something grandiose, like Napoleon or Caesar, while his mother prefers something more ordinary. They argue back and forth without agreement until one or the other, or perhaps both simultaneously, catches sight of the little dog's tail, like a pompom chrysanthemum in bloom, and in the same breath, they shout 'Pompom!' It is an unusual and pretty name, which Pompom learns in no time at all. When Huanhuan calls her, she gets up, and the boy sweeps her up into his arms and onto the bed. Then Pompom rolls round and round like a little bundle of fluff. She has another trick too: she sneaks up on tiptoes, stops when she is near enough, then launches herself at him, pressing her head against his face and licking him from his forehead right down to his chin. The scene plays itself out again and again, with Huanhuan lavishing all sorts of nicknames on the dog: 'Good Girl, Chubby Baby, Cutie-Pie, my little Michael Jackson.' Hezi has never known her son so smitten and, as she does the washing-up and listens to their play, it seems to her that the house feels livelier than it ever has, and the habitual melancholy of her expression softens into a smile.

Hezi has a long face, rather like a Manchu. She was very pretty in her youth, but with age her expression has become somber. Still, every now and then, if a smile should happen to cross her features, her face lights up and she looks like a different person. A middle school teacher, Hezi is in her early thirties and, since her divorce, has made sure to live a decent life and repress her emotions. Her son is her whole world, and when he is happy it brightens her day. She may not like dogs, but for his sake she puts up with Pompom.

It is getting late and time to find somewhere for Pompom to sleep. Hezi gets out an old cardboard box, lines it with some cotton wadding and puts it out on the balcony. She is fussy about cleanliness. Soon after Pompom arrives, she sees that the dog has some crud in its eyes and suggests to Huanhuan that it needs a bath. Pompom is very docile and doesn't struggle at all. Once it is washed, they wrap it in a towel and dry it with the blow dryer till its coat is all fluffy again. Then Pompom suddenly starts shivering uncontrollably, froths at the mouth, and has an attack of diarrhea. Huanhuan bursts into torrents of tears and points an accusing finger at his mother. 'It's all your fault!' he yells. 'You hurt her!' Finally, he shuts himself in the bathroom and carries on choking with sobs. 'Pompom is going to die! My Pompom is going to die!'

Hezi forces herself to be calm but inwardly she is terrified. Then she looks at this bundle of fluff that is shrinking away by the minute and pulls herself together. It is time for desperate measures. She'll try what worked when Huanhuan was ill as a baby. She gets some antibiotics and cold remedy pills, grinds up two of each, and mixes them up together. Gripping the puppy firmly, she spoons the mixture into its mouth. Pompom gives a squeal like a child and struggles so hard that only half goes in. By this time, Hezi is sweating profusely. She wraps the puppy in an old quilt of Huanhuan's and tucks her into the cardbox box on the balcony. When she goes in to see her son, he has gone to sleep.

Hezi, however, lies wide awake. *Damn it!* she thinks. Whoever would imagine that such a tiny thing could be such a worry. As the night wears on, the wind gets up and the curtains flap and cast fretwork shadows on the wall opposite the bed. Hezi stares, watching the shadows change shape, and she quails inwardly as if she has committed some terrible misdeed. Finally, out of the darkness, she hears a shrill cry. Could it really be the dog? And all this time she'd thought dogs could only bark. Quietly, she creeps out and sees a bundle of white fur and a pair of bright eyes looking at her in the darkness.

'Pompom?' she says. The little bundle gets to its feet, and clutches her leg with its paws. She is suddenly overwhelmed with sadness. Such a tiny, vulnerable creature, with no one in this world except herself and her son to look after it. She picks it up in her arms, feeling its warm soft fur, and it presses its face hard to hers. *Mum! I'm better! Pompom* seems to be saying.

From then on, it is as if she has a daughter. First thing in the morning, Pompom sneaks into her room, jumps on her bed and licks her awake. This is the signal that it is time for their morning walk. Hezi: 'Out?' The dog cocks her head. Hezi, teasingly: 'Where's your leash?' The dog gives a little jump and cocks her head the other way. Hezi can't repress a chuckle. Pompom knows that the leash means a walk. Hezi has spent seventy yuan at the pet shop on a dog leash; all their stuff is very expensive. They clearly have a wealthy clientele and everything is priced accordingly. Hezi's salary is enough for her and her son to get by well enough, but a dog on top of that? Every city dog needs a permit, which costs five thousand yuan. And then there are the rules and regulations. Dog-walking is permitted only before 7 am and after 8 pm, which means walking in the pitch darkness in winter. Hezi can't afford the permit yet. But, on their walks, she discovers that almost none of the owners have bought their dogs permits and gradually her fears quieten.

The pollution in Beijing gets steadily worse. The city is one big building site with all the attendant noise and traffic jams and less and less residential space. Every corner now sprouts traffic lights, but they do nothing to control the streams of cars and pedestrians. Hezi's complex used to have a patch of grass in front of it. Half of this is now occupied by a construction site, and soon they'll be chopping down the canopy of trees to erect workmen's huts. Dust from the reinforced concrete fills the air and mixes with exhaust fumes. Even the grass turns grey. Hezi is hard pressed to find somewhere to take Pompom for her walk. Her pretty white fur turns grey, with streaks of black showing through. Only her tongue remains the same vivid pink as before.

It is hard to avoid making comparisons between the local dogs. There is Lili, a bitch belonging to a family whose house has been demolished, not nearly as attractive as Pompom. Then there is Qiuqiu, Maomao and Tiaotiao in the building behind them, all of them mongrel Pekinese-type mutts, nothing out of the ordinary. Carl, on the twelfth floor, is an attractive dog, with the same pure white fur as Pompom. He's a pedigree shih tzu, an aristocrat among small dogs, but is getting on in years. Otherwise he would make a good mate for Pompom. Hezi has been looking for a suitable match for some time and isn't quite sure what she feels about her lack of success: perhaps disappointment mixed with pride, and a delicious feeling that it will just be the three of them. Huanhuan has no such worries; he buys popsicles when he takes Pompom out, attracting all the neighborhood dogs around them. They soon get to know the dog owners too. The only one who annoys Hezi is Carl's owner. He is a manager of a local restaurant, a man of means. His dog is a cut above the others, and he is inordinately proud of him. Every time the dog raises his head, the owner pours a little from the mineral water bottle he carries into his cupped palm and holds it out for Carl to drink. He even sprays Carl with it in hot weather to cool him down. He may think this is the way the upper class behave, but in Hezi's view he is simply being pretentious.

One night in the middle of summer, Hezi showers and puts on a flowery polyester sleeveless top and loose trousers to take Pompom for a walk. She has left it till late deliberately so as to avoid other people. As luck would have it, she bumps right into Carl's owner. Intent on giving them a wide berth, Hezi tugs on the leash, but Carl and Pompom have other ideas. They are instantly fascinated by each other and begin rubbing noses and nipping playfully. There is no pulling them away. Carl's owner glances sidelong at Pompom. 'Not bad, your dog,' he concedes. 'What's its name?' As though this is the first time he has seen her.

Hezi feels a flash of anger. 'Well, of course, a great man like you would hardly remember the time when Carl begged a popsicle off our Huanhuan.'

'Oh, oh, yes of course,' says Carl's owner. 'It's Pompom, isn't it? And what breed is it? It doesn't look Pekinese.'

'Of course she's not Pekinese,' said Hezi, chin in air. 'She's a German Pomeranian, a rare breed.' In fact, Hezi has no idea whether Pompom is a Pomeranian, but she is quite sure she wants to bring Carl's owner down a peg or two.

The man is astonished. 'Really? A German Pomeranian?! Here, Pompom, do a little trot for me!' Pompom trots obligingly. She looks like a cloud come alive, seeming to fly. Carl can't catch up with her no matter how hard he tries. His owner's eyes sparkle. 'She really is a Pomeranian. Good heavens, Pomeranians make wonderful pets. When she's grown, she'll be able to do all sorts of stuff around the house for you!'

'Really!' responds Hezi with a show of indifference.

The man talks on and on, showing off his knowledge of dogs. 'German Pomeranians are lively, cute, loyal and brave, big-hearted, take up hardly any space, and have no shortcomings at all… Besides, we are the only two with pedigree dogs around here… May I ask, how old is Pompom?'

Hezi tugs at Pompom's leash. 'She's just a puppy,' she says and stalks away.

'Well, don't let her turn into an old maid like that Lili!' Carl's owner shouts after her.

Hezi doesn't turn around, but she says to herself, *And so what if she does? We'll never let her mate with an old mutt like Carl!* A moment later, she can't help laughing out loud. It has suddenly occurred to her how much younger she feels, and how much happier, since they got Pompom.

When they get home, Huanhuan is washing his feet. He looks at her and pouts. 'I think you love Pompom more than me, Mum!' Hezi takes off the dog's leash and refills her bowl with fresh water. Pompom pounces on it and glugs it down.

Hezi is all smiles as she watches her. 'Don't be silly. You're my son, she's just a dog. There's no comparison. What a terrible thing to say!'

'Still, since she came, you haven't paid nearly as much attention to me,' Huanhuan mutters.

'Then let's get rid of her! Or turn her into a stew! Red-cooked with soy sauce!' Laughing, she goes to the kitchen to prepare some pork spareribs.

Huanhuan's mouth turns down even harder. 'You won't treat yourself to ribs, but you give them to the dog to eat. How's that not favoritism?'

'You two eat the ribs,' says Hezi. 'Puppies and boys need extra calcium. It'd be a lot of trouble if you got soft bones.' They chat away until the ribs are ready. By the time Hezi has tidied away Huanhuan's schoolbag and given Pompom a late night snack, it is midnight. Finally getting into bed, Hezi grabs the *Encyclopedia of Dogs* and begins to read. She is determined to become an expert in pet care.

From then on, Hezi and Carl's owner meet up from time to time. Outwardly aloof, they are secretly competitive when it comes to the dogs. For instance, Carl's owner will sit on a stone pillar and take his shoe off and throw it. 'Carl, fetch!' he commands. And the dog, with his ungainly run, fetches the shoe back.

Hezi's lips turn into a pout. 'That's nothing special. And besides, it's rude to throw shoes in public. The sort of thing a country hick does.' She commands Pompom to fetch her leash and Pompom duly obeys. She is nimbler and prettier than Carl.

Annoyed, Carl's owner turns to go, but before he does so he gives Carl another command. 'Say goodbye to Pompom!' And Carl stands on his hind legs and raises his forepaws in the air as if waving goodbye.

Hezi is not going down without a fight. 'Say byebye to Carl!' she commands Pompom, and Pompom stands on her hind legs, paws clasped to her chest in the traditional Chinese salutation.

Carl's owner cannot repress a smile. 'Good girl,' he mutters before walking off.

In no time at all, it is autumn. National Day, October 1st, this year will mark the fifty-fifth anniversary of the founding of New China. Beijing empties as everyone goes back to their homes for the holidays. The city seems suddenly bigger and more spacious, quieter and brighter. A rainstorm scours the leaves and grass clean and restores them to their former green. Not far into the new term at Huanhuan and Hezi's school, Hezi receives a prize for being a model teacher in their community. With her bonus, she plans to buy the dog license for Pompom. But when she eventually finds a spare moment and goes to the office, she is told they are shut until next May or June, and she should come back then.

Pompom is no longer a puppy. She weighs ten pounds now and has a long white coat and black lustrous eyes. She is a very cute dog. She no longer sleeps on the balcony or even on the sofa. Only a bed is good enough for her, either Hezi's or Huanhuan's, and she makes sure to distribute her favors equally. If mother and son are sitting together, she squeezes in between them. She is a good guard dog, barking as soon as a stranger approaches along the walkway. But she never barks at Hezi or Huanhuan. Instead, if she wants to communicate something to them, she emits delicate little chattering noises. It is the kind of sound a dumb person who has had some success with acupuncture treatment might make, Hezi thinks. Slightly squeaky, a sort of Chinese coloratura soprano.

'She can almost talk,' says Huanhuan. 'Wouldn't it be great if she spoke like a human one day? She'd get into the *Guinness Book of Records*!'

'I wouldn't be at all surprised if she spoke,' says Hezi. 'She's more human than dog.' They laugh. Pompom has come into season once

– as Hezi finds out from the encyclopedia, bitches come into season twice a year and should only become pregnant after the third time, so Hezi makes sure to keep a close eye on her 'daughter' for the time being.

One evening, Pompom makes it clear she wants to go out. No sooner have they stepped out of the building and got to the corner than Hezi hears someone say in a low voice, 'Take Pompom back inside, quick!' In astonishment, she turns and sees Carl's owner, staring at her with a blank expression on his face. 'Something terrible's happened. Carl's been taken. Go back in!'

Hezi scurries back home with Pompom in her arms. When Huanhuan learns what happened to Carl, he goes downstairs. He comes back shortly, puffing and panting. 'They're doing an inspection before National Day. Carl went out half an hour too early and the dog patrol snatched him!' Hezi clutches Pompom in fright. She feels desperately sorry for Carl's owner. To think that Carl was snatched because he went out half an hour too early, even though he had a dog license! It would be disastrous if Pompom were taken. She discusses it with Huanhuan and they decide the best thing is to take Pompom to an aunt who lives in the countryside, just until National Day is over.

That night, Hezi looks at her son, tucked snugly in bed with Pompom. She cannot sleep. She creeps downstairs. Outside, on the patch of grass she goes to so often, she sees the glimmer of a lit cigarette in the darkness. Carl's owner is there smoking. This normally vigorous restaurateur does his best to give an impression of calmness but seems suddenly to have shrunk in stature, and Hezi feels a flicker of pity. She crosses to where he stands and asks if there is any news about Carl. 'I've just come from the dog patrol office,' he says, dragging deeply on his cigarette. 'It's okay, I'll get him back tomorrow morning. I just have to pay a fine. But I'd advise you to get Pompom out of the city for a while, keep her out of the way. Apparently, they're checking dogs daily until National Day, going house to house, checking up on licenses. Any dogs without a license will be taken and sold to a vivisection laboratory… And even the dogs that don't end up there are going to have a hard time.'

'Is Carl having a hard time?'

He sighs. 'I just went to take a look. All the dogs the patrol has seized have been taken to a warehouse. There were a thousand or more in there, all barking away. The lad in charge got so frantic, he turned the pressure hose on the whole lot of them. By the time I got there, there wasn't a bark to be heard. It was pitch-dark and they were all huddled around a bowl of filthy water… How terrible for little Carl!' In spite of his best efforts, the man's voice cracks and his eyes swim with tears.

Hezi feels tears come to her eyes too. 'Really! What harm has a little dog like him done to anyone?! But don't torture yourself thinking about it. You go home and get a good rest. I'm so grateful for what you did today…'

Carl's owner waves her thanks away: 'It's just what neighbors do. You go back in, I'll stay here for a bit. I won't sleep even if I do go home. Besides, my wife and daughter are both crying their eyes out and I can't bear it!'

That weekend, Hezi gets a friend to take her and Pompom to Changping, on the outskirts of Beijing, where an aunt of hers lives. It is like sending a daughter off with a trousseau: Pompom goes with her favorite fried fish, doggie chocolate, beef jerky and frankfurters, and when they arrive, Hezi makes a point of offering her aunt's dogs some of the chocolate, so that Pompom can start off on the right foot with them. To her surprise, the dogs won't go near the chocolate. The bitch is in pup, but she only has some leftover noodles in her bowl and a bit more tomato than the other dogs. Her aunt smiles. 'They've never had chocolate before, it's wasted on them!' There are four dogs, a German shepherd, a Beauceron, and two shih tzus, Dumbdumb and Jewel, who is the one in pup. Hezi is relieved to note that they are not actively hostile to Pompom, though they are not overly friendly either. They just sniff, wag their tails and leave her alone – except for Dumbdumb, who chases around after Pompom with great enthusiasm, until the aunt shouts angrily at him, 'Heartless wretch, your mate is carrying your pups and you're already infatuated with another female!'

There is general laughter at her jibe, and Hezi laughs along. 'Dumbdumb's not dumb at all!' She leaves the homestead in a cheerful mood, but things change on the way home. Huanhuan is sitting beside her friend in the passenger seat, his head bent. From the back seat, Hezi can see only his trouser leg, on which there seems to be a patch of dampness, a patch that gets bigger and bigger, until he cannot hold back the sobs any longer. Hezi feels her own eyes well with tears. She is quite desolate at the thought of that shaggy, warm little body with her soft-as-velvet coat. She would feel so much better if she could cuddle Pompom right now.

It is with some trepidation that she calls them that evening, but her aunt's loud tones reassure Hezi and Huanhuan. 'She's doing fine. She hasn't eaten much, but lots of dogs are like that when they go to a strange place. Give it a bit of time. She won't hold out more than four or five days, you'll see!'

The next day Hezi calls again. Her aunt is quieter this time. 'She's still not eating, but don't you worry. Dumbdumb and Jewel were like this when they first came here! I know all about dogs.'

'Please, Aunt,' Hezi says meekly. 'Do what you can to tempt her to eat, try anything!' Her aunt tells her not to worry, but Hezi does not feel confident.

On the third day, Hezi has to make a work trip to Xi'an. She tries repeatedly to call her aunt before she leaves but cannot get through. On tenterhooks, she leaves for Xi'an. Early the next morning she has a dream. Pompom, her long silvery coat blown by the wind, is tearing along like a tornado, running through clouds until she gets to Hezi's feet and suddenly stops. She put her claws on Hezi's leg and bursts out in human language: 'Mum! I miss you!' Hezi starts awake in terror, and stares blankly out of the window at the dawn sky.

Hezi is home after a week. It is Sunday, Huanhuan is not there, and the house is in a terrible mess. Mechanically, Hezi begins to tidy up, feeling increasingly flustered. At noon, the shrill sound of the telephone startles her so much that she trembles. It takes her a minute to pick up. It is her aunt, but Hezi can hear nothing except a droning noise, like a bellow. She remembers nothing after that, not even how she manages to get to her aunt's house, though it seems to take an awfully long time, changing from one bus to another to another, and costs her a lot of money. The night is drawing in by the time she arrives. The whole family is there, and so is Huanhuan, his eyes frightfully swollen. Her aunt is in tears. 'I've had dogs, so many dogs, but I've never known one so stubborn. Pompom just refused to eat, and if you forced it down her, she spat it out, and every night she barked and barked in the direction of your house. The first couple of days I thought she'd be okay, but the third day I got scared and tried calling you but no one picked up. I called your school and they said you'd gone on a trip and would be back in a few days. I honestly had no idea… But what a faithful dog she was! She wasn't just an ordinary pet, she was really special… I'm so sorry, I'm so sorry!… But how about this? Jewel's due to have her puppies in a couple of days. Why don't you pick one of them? I know it won't be as good as Pompom, but it'll be a pedigree shih tzu. It would be something, wouldn't it?'

Hezi has no idea whether she nodded or not. She holds Huanhuan's hand and her aunt and her family take them to see Pompom's grave. Her aunt tells them the site has very good *fengshui*, with mountains on one side and water on the other. Hezi and Huanhuan pick a bunch of wildflowers and place them on the tiny grave. Huanhuan keeps on crying until he has cried himself hoarse. Hezi does not shed a single tear, just stares blankly, making no attempt to comfort her son or to speak at all.

After October 1st is over, the aunt really does bring them a puppy. It is very pretty, with a long silvery coat like Pompom. In fact it looks like Pompom when she first arrived, with the same ungainly gait. They call it Baobao. That evening, Hezi takes the puppy downstairs for a breath of fresh air. All the dogs who were corralled are back with their owners now, but she cannot see Carl. Finally, when it is getting dark, Carl's owner emerges, looking wretched.

'Where's Carl?' asks Hezi.

There is a long silence. 'When he was taken away, he lost the use of his legs…'

'Make them compensate you!'

'Never mind that, it wouldn't be enough! They fined me three thousand, plus the license is five thousand, so that was eight thousand before they handed Carl over.'

'You mean Carl didn't have a license?'

'Oh, he did, but it was from Tongxian so it didn't count. You'd better take good care of that pretty little thing you've got! Is it Pompom's puppy?'

Hezi forces herself to nod. 'Yes, she is pretty, isn't she?' she says.

Carl's owner cannot take his eyes off Baobao and Hezi thinks she sees tears. 'If only Carl hadn't been injured so badly… Ai! Laugh if you want, but when I went to fetch him home, I was broken-hearted…' And suddenly he bursts into loud sobs. A grown man, bawling like a child.

Hezi cannot explain why she lied to Carl's owner. The truth is that she hardly dares face the fact that Pompom has died. When the restaurateur wept, she could not cry, she did not want to blub along with him. But now, in the depths of the night, she cannot hold back the tears any longer. Pompom, that beautiful, lovable dog who did no harm to anyone, is dead because she was too faithful, too devoted to her owners. And it was a willed death; she was so steadfast, there was nothing casual about it. It was a pure life and a clean death, Hezi thinks. And Pompom was much stronger in her resolve than Hezi, who drifts through life, come what may. The flood gates open and a torrent of tears come.

After a little while, she feels a warm fluffy thing crawl onto her face and lick the tears with its delicate little tongue. She reaches out and takes this small living creature in her arms. Such a vulnerable creature. It will meet so many hazards in its life, but she determines to protect it with all her might. It is only a dog but it deserves to be treated well. She hopes Baobao will have better luck than Pompom. And with that thought, she falls into a deep sleep.

In her dream, she sees the red flare of twilight and a swath of white flowers, a small white dog leaping among them. At first glance it looks like Pompom. But no, she looks closer and it is Baobao. She flings herself towards it. Try as she might, though, it is always beyond her reach. Then the red flare and the white flowers turn into a screen in which Pompom, Baobao, Carl, Dumbdumb and Jewels, Lili and Qiuqiu all swirl in a dance, as if in a slow-motion film, and she smiles in her dream. At that instant, Baobao wakes up, opens his lustrous dark eyes and looks curiously at his mistress's face. However does she manage to smile through her tears? That is something this little pup will never master, not in a lifetime of trying.

Miss Asia

As far as Qiao Xi was concerned, every Sunday afternoon was a good afternoon. This was when her husband went out to the supermarket and she was free to nap just as much as she pleased, sleeping right through to four or five o'clock. Getting fat didn't bother her – her husband was as fat as the Laughing Buddha and her son as lumpen as a steelyard, and beside them she was positively slender, despite being approximately twenty-five percent heavier than she should be. Besides, she had a stable job and a happy marriage. She had just been promoted to assistant head of the Film and Television Production Department and Da Geng, her husband, was well-known for his honesty; there was no need to worry about him playing around and absolutely no reason to agonise over losing weight.

Generally, she considered someone who interrupted her nap to be the very worst kind of person. When her eyes snapped open at the sound of the doorbell, she stumbled over to the door, tripping on a pair of slippers as she opened it. For a moment, she felt blinded – she'd emerged from a dimly-lit bedroom and the figure that awaited her was a dazzling sight: at least one metre seventy tall, a waist that couldn't have been more than twenty inches all round, hair highlighted with two vivid swathes of maroon. A cropped gold jacket over a long dress of ivory brocade and, on her feet, a pair of maroon high heels, complementing the gleam of her hair. In all honesty, had the girl been a little less sophisticated, or her skin a little less fair, she would never have pulled it off. But she was so chic and her skin so white that it was a while before Qiao Xi even noticed that there was someone else standing behind her. A woman, bright-eyed, her eyebrows elegantly slanted. Attractive enough, but nowhere near as beautiful as the girl. Qiao Xi recognised her from somewhere.

'Hurry up and say hello to your auntie! My goodness, this child's slow off the mark,' said the woman, and Qiao Xi realised that this must be He Xiangxiang, the wife of one of her younger cousins.

She hadn't heard from her in years. Something must have happened, for her to be turning up out of the blue like this.

'Hello, Auntie,' said the girl, and as she did so Qiao Xi noticed that not a flicker of movement crossed her beautiful face; it remained entirely expressionless. *So she's one of those wooden beauties*, thought Qiao Xi.

She invited them in and brewed some tea. Pu'er tea, which she sipped at carefully. She didn't usually pay much attention to tea, but the Pu'er had been tucked away in the outside store cupboard ever since someone gave it to her as a gift, and she was worried it might be mouldy. There'd been a whiff of rot as she pulled out a bit for the teapot.

'I've a bad head for names – this is...' She glanced at the girl.

'Oh, no wonder you don't remember! You haven't seen this one since she was eight or nine, back when her daddy was still alive,' said He Xiangxiang, not forgetting to choke up a little over 'her daddy'. Qiao Xi's cousin, Yang Ping, had died in a car crash, and He Xiangxiang had never remarried. 'This is Daffodil!'

'Daffodil!' exclaimed Qiao Xi, pressing a cup of tea into the girl's pale, slender hands, then clasping them in her own. Daffodil's face remained completely impassive.

Hurriedly, He Xiangxiang spoke up. 'Would you look at this child!

Talking non-stop every day about her auntie, and now we're here she can't get a word out. Too shy for her own good, that's what she is.'

They picked up their respective cups, blew, and Qiao Xi suddenly recalled that her cousin had indeed had a daughter. Stunning, even as a child, and here she was, all grown up. A good figure, but the contours of her face had changed and weren't as beautiful as before. She had been at primary school when they last met, and twenty years had passed in a flash, making her around thirty. A decade or so earlier, Qiao Xi had heard she went to Hong Kong for the Miss Asia competition. She came second and signed on with some kind of agency, went into show business, fell out of touch. There was no special occasion warranting a visit, so what was she doing here? Knowing He Xiangxiang, there would be a reason behind it. Qiao Xi came to a decision: she wouldn't say anything, just smile and drink her tea.

As expected, after a few moments of silence, He Xiangxiang caved in. She stood up and presented Qiao Xi with a gift. Upon opening it, Qiao Xi's first reaction was shock: four perfect sticks of glistening yellow. Not gold, surely – but then again, what else could it be?

He Xiangxiang had her eyes nervously lowered and did not see Qiao Xi's pupils as they grew almost frighteningly large. She bowed deferentially, her face a little flushed, but eventually found her tongue. 'Oh, sister, just a little thing, a token of our gratitude.... I know you're a busy lady, with a household to run, so I'll get right to the point. We're here today because of this silly girl!'

She made as though to jab Daffodil in the forehead, snatching her hand back when it was two centimetres away, as if afraid of injuring that fragile skin and the tender flesh beneath.

'Daffodil is her pet name, Susan is her English name. After the beauty contest she went to America, and that's what everyone started calling her. This child! She'll be the death of me!'

She stopped talking and instead just sat there, weeping noisily.

Qiao Xi hurriedly passed her a tissue. 'Xiangxiang, what are you talking about? Daffodil looks wonderful! The only difference from the last time I saw her is that she's grown a bit since then.' She gestured towards Daffodil. 'And even as a young thing, you could tell she was something special. Didn't she win Miss Asia ten years ago, and then sign on with a modelling agency? It sounds like she's doing fine! What's all this fuss about?'

The box containing the gold bars was wide open, glittering forlornly, ignored by everyone in the room. Daffodil – or rather, *Susan* – sat quietly to one side of it, face perfectly expressionless, as though oblivious to the tragicomedy playing out before her.

He Xiangxiang began to recount the tale. Her words were measured, well-reasoned, to the point. This was exactly the kind of rehearsed speech that Qiao Xi loathed. Not a single hole in the logic! It put her in a terrible mood. She had a natural inclination towards picking out the flaws in other people's arguments and then correcting them; schooling them. This performance was watertight, and she found it impossibly dull.

She understood, of course. It was more or less as she'd expected: could she get Daffodil an in with her production team, set up her with a part. Just a bit part would be fine, according to the words on He Xiangxiang's lips, but the shiny gold bars told another story. At the very least the supporting lady, they said – but preferably the lead.

He Xiangxiang's outpouring was full of implied meanings. *Daffodil was so silly, couldn't handle interpersonal relationships, couldn't pick up on facial cues.* And Qiao Xi knew what she was really saying: Daffodil was pure and innocent, unsullied, didn't play by the unwritten rules of the entertainment world.

Qiao Xi kept glancing at Daffodil from the corner of her eyes. In terms of looks, she was at least on a par with an early career Fan Bingbing, back during her *My Fair Princess* days. Daffodil's face was a little more wooden, although perhaps they could train that out of her. But her whole bearing was so very un-Chinese, and there was no escaping the Hong Kong twang to her speech, or the fact she had no formal training. All of which seemed likely to limit her chances. Qiao Xi drew her brows together, as though deep in contemplation, and at just that moment Da Geng arrived home, weighed down with Walmart shopping bags.

As they exchanged greetings, Qiao Xi noticed a hint of a smile on the wooden beauty's face. A tiny flicker, her upper lip tilting slightly upwards at the edges, and it dawned on Qiao Xi that it was an attempt to prevent wrinkles. Miss Asia from ten years ago – even if Daffodil had launched her career at eighteen, that would still make her twenty-eight. And Qiao Xi clearly recalled her being quite a lot older than eighteen when she received her crown. Ah, age would certainly be a problem! Qiao Xi's eyes suddenly lit up, and beneath the intense beam of her gaze, the light in Daffodil's eyes went dim.

'How old is she?' asked Qiao Xi, getting straight to the point.

He Xiangxiang reddened, as though exposed in a lie. 'Aiyo! Sister, what a question! She started her career so early...'

Qiao Xi briskly cut her off. 'Let her speak for herself!'

The wooden beauty stared at this plump relative of hers in shock, her lips forming a perfect 'O'. When she spoke, it was an astronomical figure: thirty-one. A pause. And then she erupted, 'Oh, Auntie! Please help me!' Instantly, tears welled up – nothing overly dramatic, just enough to swim in her eyes; a woeful picture.

'I so want to act! Even if I have to do it for free... I, I...', her voice was choked with emotion. 'I know I'm a bit older, but look at me, I don't look that old, and with some make-up, I'm still...'

As she spoke, she looked directly at Qiao Xi, and her thoroughly unrehearsed approach struck a chord. There was more sincerity to her few, halting sentences than to all of He Xiangxiang's smooth patter. Having the upper hand was Qiao Xi's favourite thing in the world, and seeing Miss Asia humbled before her like this, she was quick to agree: 'Hush, child, calm down! Of course I'll help.'

Then she insisted on returning the gold bars to He Xiangxiang, reasoning that she had not yet done anything to deserve them.

'Wait until I've actually helped,' she said. 'Then you can thank me.'

The box went back and forth between their two pairs of aging hands, before finally returning to its original owner. The gift had not been given, which made He Xiangxiang understandably nervous. But Qiao Xi felt sure of her decision: if she accepted, He Xiangxiang would be harassing her with phone calls a hundred times a day, and she'd have no right to resent it. Having rejected the gift, she was in charge. Now, she could help if she wanted and not if she didn't, and no one could make her do otherwise!

Some of Daffodil's old luck must have stayed with her. Not long after their meeting, Qiao Xi heard that the station was putting together a new show. They'd had a big-name actress lined up to play the part of a conniving young heiress, but in the end she couldn't free the time in her schedule. With the rest of the cast and crew already assembled, they were in desperate need of a replacement.

'This heiress is the main supporting female. She spends the whole forty-episode run trying to kill the leading lady, so there's a decent amount of screen-time,' an assistant informed Qiao Xi. Qiao Xi called the director that same day and arranged for Daffodil to audition the next.

On the phone, He Xiangxiang gushed with thanks. But early the next morning, her delight had turned to tears. 'I don't know what to do,' she sobbed. 'Daffodil went on a trip to Hong Kong, and I can't get hold of her!'

Qiao Xi was stunned for a moment, and then firm. 'Well, I'm afraid I can't help you there.'

There was a quiet click as she hung up.

Once again, fortune sided with Daffodil. At the very last minute, two days before they were due to start filming, she finally showed up for her audition, jittery with nerves. But the audition was just a formality – had they been in a position to choose, they would never have hired someone older than thirty. She had done all sorts to maintain her face (IPL skin rejuvenation, anti-wrinkle electrotherapy, traditional treatments to get rid of freckles and dark spots) and layered on foundation, but when it came down to it, she simply couldn't compete with girls in their teens or early twenties. Instead, she had to rely on her body. Not being well-endowed in the breast department, she had gone the skinny route. She had a long fringe covering her forehead, hair extensions, and wore a cream velvet coat to the appointment, over long cream boots with four-inch heels. Beneath all that, she really did exude an ethereal, waif-like beauty.

Due to Qiao Xi's connections, Hong Bao, the director, voiced no objection to having Daffodil come on board. A few days later, the cast and crew left to start filming in Zhuhai, taking her with them. At long last, He Xiangxiang could breathe a sigh of relief. Every now and then she would drop in on Qiao Xi, and of course she never arrived empty-handed. Only, to her bemusement, Qiao Xi continued to refuse her gifts.

Qiao Xi did not wish ill of He Xiangxiang, although neither did she feel particularly warm towards her. But women of their age, however full and happy their lives, often harbour a nagging sense of loneliness. On one of her visits, He Xiangxiang succeeded in convincing Qiao Xi to come shopping – the sales were on, and even top brands like Prada, Armani, Chanel and Versace had discounts, not to mention the second- and third-rate labels.

How long had it been since Qiao Xi was last in a shopping mall? Everyone has their regrets: single people lament their lack of family, and married people mourn their freedom. Freedom is not so simple as you might think. For years, Qiao Xi had lived a comfortable existence, but she'd forgotten what freedom felt like. And here she was in her fifties, being dragged all over the brand-new Golden Resources shopping mall by He Xiangxiang, catching a glimpse of a different kind of life. There was something to be said for it.

They were ecstatic to discover a shop selling off stock with discounts of up to ninety percent. The second they entered, He Xiangxiang turned quick and nimble as a leopardess, her eyes settling instantly on a spring dress for Qiao Xi. It was made from a natural ramie fibre, beige, the sleeves and collar picked out in pale-pink linen. The collar was intricately embroidered with tiny grapes, linked by dark grey vines. It was undeniably gorgeous. He Xiangxiang shoved Qiao Xi into a changing room. Seeing herself in the mirror, Qiao Xi was startled – where had all this pasty white flesh sprung from? And that belly like a strung-up pig's intestine, hanging in wobbly folds... how could anything look good on such a body?

But it did. She couldn't believe it! With the dress on, her imperfections vanished. She twirled this way and that, examining herself in the dressing room mirror, and then stepped out to twirl this way and that in front of He Xiangxiang and the sales assistant. As they cooed with admiration, she made up her mind to buy it. A direct French import, originally four thousand yuan, now reduced to five hundred – but before she had even made it to the sales counter, He Xiangxiang came over clutching the receipt.

'Oh, you shouldn't have!' said Qiao Xi, although inside she was pleased. Then He Xiangxiang took her for a paraffin wax hand treatment, a decorative manicure and, to top it all off, an ice cream in Häagen-Dazs. All He Xiangxiang's treat, of course. Qiao Xi eyed her bulging wallet, packed with cards; several dozen, at the very least.

'What a life, Xiangxiang!' said Qiao Xi, scraping the pale surface of her green tea ice cream with a tiny spoon. And then, as though it were just an after-thought, 'You must be doing pretty well for yourself?'

He Xiangxiang's eyes were like a pair of dyed glass beads, faded a long way past the brilliant amber of their youth. 'For myself? Oh, I don't mind telling you, my dear, that Daffodil earned every dime!'

Qiao Xi stared in surprise.

'It's ten years since she was selected for Miss Asia, and after she won second place and the award for Miss Most Photogenic, she was snapped up by Pershing Management. She had all sorts of roles. Plus, I lived very frugally, and had a certain amount of savings... She never made it big, but I told you about that. Nowadays, everyone knows how it works in show business, all those unwritten rules, but back when Daffodil was starting out...Oh, the child suffered unbelievable hardships!'

Qiao Xi was unmoved. 'There may be unwritten rules, but if her acting's up to the mark, then a show's a show, and there's no reason she shouldn't make it with this one. Ultimately, it's up to the viewers to decide! Once she's finished shooting, I'd recommend that she go to acting school for a bit. Just a suggestion, but...'

'Yes, yes, good idea! Then we won't need to keep on bothering you, will we?'

Qiao Xi coughed slightly, as though a chunk of unblended ice from her ice cream had snagged in her throat.

They took their time over the desserts, chatting as they ate. Qiao Xi discovered that, soon after Daffodil signed the Pershing contract, He Xiangxiang and her husband had gone to join her in America. They thought this was it, her big break. Little did they know, a few parts down the line, not only would Daffodil still be practically unknown, she would have a disastrous falling-out with her management. Following which she would flee the entertainment world and move in with her parents. Except, after life in show business, how was she supposed to go back to being an ordinary person again? There was no denying that she was stunningly beautiful, and members of the Los Angeles Chinese community were forever asking her to host things, which gave her a bit of income. But that money would only stretch so far, and Yang Ping began plotting his daughter's Hollywood takeover. But how to go about it? Think of how many Chinese actresses wasted their whole lives attempting that very same thing, to no avail. Even if they took off every stitch of clothing, they still couldn't compete with those other girls – girls who wouldn't even give you the time of day, who were so brazen that they didn't just sleep their way in, they actually paid money for the privilege. And even then, all they ended up with was a thin stream of bit parts, playing the butt of some racist joke about Chinese people, completely forgetting who their ancestors were.

Yang Ping thought he knew a thing or two about working connections. By channelling years of savings in the right direction, he managed to secure Daffodil a meeting with a Hollywood producer. The producer in question was an American with British roots, supposedly with links to the aristocracy – rumour had it that an ancestor had been a trusted advisor to Queen Elizabeth the First. The man's cheeks and nose were ruddy, and the backs of his hands mottled with age spots. When he arrived at the meeting and caught sight of those hands, Yang Ping felt himself relax. The man asked a few questions, then had Daffodil do a couple of simple performances. After watching her, he furrowed his brow and mumbled something to himself. Yang Ping asked him to repeat it, and the man said simply, 'Your daughter is still young, there is absolutely nothing stopping her from spending a little time studying television performance.'

Yang Ping knew this was a tactful criticism of Daffodil's acting, but he couldn't bring himself to accept it. Creasing his whole face into a smile, he presented the director with the enormous pile of gifts he had brought with him. At the sight of which, the director instinctively recoiled, bumping against the back of his chair. Then, muttering an apology, he tucked his bag under his arm and marched from the room, clearly furious.

Yang Ping dared not look at his daughter.

He was so agitated that he forgot to take the presents with him when he left – those presents that had cost him his life savings! Instead, a waiter passed them on to a stony-faced Daffodil. In the car home, Yang Ping gripped the steering wheel with trembling hands, while Daffodil was so angry that she refused to sit beside him in the passenger seat. A stroke of luck, as it turned out; a decision that would save her life. It all happened so quickly. Not long after they turned onto the road, a Volvo came racing up behind them. Yang Ping's hands were still unsteady and he forgot to indicate a turn; the Volvo was in the process of overtaking, and it slammed right into them.

Daffodil felt like she was flying, then landed heavily on the ground. Her first reaction was to clutch her head in her hands and screw her eyes shut. When she finally opened them, nothing seemed real. The blood and splattered brains all around her were like special effects from one of those Hollywood movies she was always watching.

For a long time after, Daffodil's mind was even more addled than usual. She couldn't picture her father's final moments. One moment, she thought he'd been slumped across the steering wheel; the next, she was sure he'd hurtled through the windscreen.

She remembered her mother wailing like her heart had been wrenched from her chest, and she remembered how, not long after, she'd put on a different face entirely. She did her makeup, doused herself in perfume, and clipped out of the house, handbag over her shoulder. Then she came home again, feet dragging, eyes downcast, as though performing in a tragic play – one that went on and on. Until, eventually, she returned hanging off the arm of a man. The man was tall and handsome, and dressed in designer labels from head to toe. Her mother appeared utterly besotted with him, but all he seemed to care about was money. Even Daffodil could sense that, despite her dazed condition.

During that period, her mother all but ignored her in favour of shopping. They had a bit of money, but Daffodil knew it wasn't an enormous amount – and the way her mother was spending, it wouldn't last long. He Xiangxiang always headed straight for the men's outfitters on the fourth floor of the mall, and everything she bought was top-end designer. Everything, even ties and socks. The man sported a never-ending array of new clothes. And not only clothes: every time they went out to eat, He Xiangxiang paid, and the man always ordered the most expensive items on the menu. After this had been going on for some time, Daffodil arrived home one day to hear muffled crying, followed by the slam of a door. The man emerged from the bedroom with his clothes all dishevelled, nodded nonchalantly at Daffodil, and walked calmly out of the house. Daffodil rushed in to find her mother lying half-naked on the bed, the quilt pulled over her face, sobbing.

At first, Daffodil assumed it was just an ordinary lovers' tiff. But then her mother spoke, sounding as though she might die from the heartbreak.

'The poor, poor man! All alone, with no one to look after him, and still he has his pride. Insists he doesn't want anyone's charity. He says he's leaving and that he won't come back unless he makes something of himself. But I just wanted us to be together, I never wanted any money from him! He says a man should be able to look after his woman, and he's going to make his fortune in Ohio, but how the hell's he going to do that in some dead-end place like Ohio?'

It suddenly occurred to Daffodil that, when a woman falls in love – even a shrewd, intelligent woman like her mother – she loses all reason. Her brains turn to glue. As a person with paste for brains herself, Daffodil didn't say much about it to her mother, just soothed her, weakly. Life had to go on, and it looked like they'd be surviving on almost-expired discount items from the supermarket that month.

Some months later, her mother finally seemed to wake up. 'China's been booming these past years,' she announced. 'Let's go back and join in. We'll sell the Los Angeles house and that'll make for a nice little cushion. We'll get you all set up! You're a damn sight prettier than that Xu Jinglei – if she can get famous, why shouldn't you?'

This sudden revival spurred an awakening in Daffodil, too. But by this point, she was well past her prime. She wasn't young anymore and, for an actress, youth is everything. Not that she understood this, resting as she was on her long-ago Miss Asia laurels, dreaming the same old dreams.

A year went by. Filming wrapped up on Daffodil's series. It was edited, released, ran during a prime time viewing slot and received top ratings. Qiao Xi settled into her 'high-fashion life' with He Xiangxiang.

She also became an avid viewer of Daffodil's show, forcing her family to watch each new episode. Daffodil's character was evil and manipulative, setting viewers' teeth on edge with her endless schemes to usurp the leading lady. Every day, internet message boards filled up with angry screeds on the matter. There was one sex scene in particular, where Daffodil was charming, despicable, in every way seemingly effortlessly perfect. So much so that Qiao Xi wondered whether she had been too harsh in her initial judgement.

'This acting's not bad! I didn't think she had it in her,' she commented, unable to help herself.

'Maybe it's not acting,' harrumphed her husband, watching by her side.

Privately, Qiao Xi was inclined to agree. Aloud, however, she took the opposite side, as was her custom. 'By this reasoning, are you saying that every good actor just plays themselves?'

At which her son stood up and walked out, lips curled into a sneer. She knew he was going to check the message boards. In a while, he'd come and ask her, yet again, 'Mum, why did you have to introduce us to such a first-class bitch?'

Qiao Xi was aware she was in the minority in her house. She didn't mind too much – so long as Daffodil was making a name for herself, that was what counted. The past years had been agony for He Xiangxiang, and if Daffodil were famous, it would put an end to all her woes.

After the show had been running a while, the top entertainment paper ran a front-page feature on Daffodil. The headline ran: *Ten Years On, Miss Asia Returns.*

Below was a full colour photo. Her head was slightly inclined and she was heavily made-up. Pearly-pink cheeks, violet eyeliner, black mascara, frosty purple lip gloss over silver-painted lips, metallic purple eye shadow slicked to the corners of her eyes. Jewels glued onto her nails. Hair gelled back and gleaming. She wore a platinum silk Shiatzy jacket with silver detailing, a skin-tight purple fishtail skirt, silver jewellery and a pair of ultra-high silver heels. She could easily have passed for an international supermodel.

Qiao Xi suddenly realised that she hadn't seen He Xiangxiang in quite a while. She reached for her phone to call, but the line was busy. She tried again, and this time it went through.

'Oh, I know, I saw it...' He Xiangxiang spoke in a lethargic drawl. 'Now media outlets all over the country are after her, wanting interviews, for her to come on their programmes. It's been so busy over here, I've barely had time to draw breath...but we should treat you all to dinner!'

'Oh, there's no need for that! You don't want to be bothering about dinner parties. I'm flexible at work these next couple of days, how about the two of us go shopping instead – haven't the end-of-season sales started?'

For three seconds, there was no response. And those three seconds reverberated in Qiao Xi's mind, amplifying, stretching out into three years.

'My dear, I'm afraid that these past few days...lately, I don't know why, but I've had such a headache! My brain hurts! Oh, she's doing so well, but I'm just about on my knees from it all...'

'Well, you take care of yourself, get some rest! And if you need anything, don't be afraid to call. I'll come right over.'

'Please, no need to trouble yourself! I can't thank you enough for all that you've done. Once I'm better, I'll bring Daffodil over to visit.'

Qiao Xi thought she detected a note of complacency in He Xiangxiang's tone. There was certainly none of the despair that had marked their first encounter.

'You must try some of this!'

They were in a well-known western restaurant. He Xiangxiang had ordered a whole table's worth of food and opened some champagne. The wooden beauty was a wooden beauty no longer: her eyes sparkled as they roved the room, and her every gesture seemed underscored with pride. She poured the wine and, as she did so, Qiao Xi noticed an extra ring adorning her pale, slender fingers. A platinum band inlaid with sapphires.

'Daffodil, I keep forgetting to ask,' she said, 'have you found yourself a nice man yet? A gorgeous girl like you must have men chasing after her!'

As she spoke, Qiao Xi's thoughts turned to her chubby, perpetually single son.

Astutely, He Xiangxiang stepped in to answer. 'Well, of course they chase but, hard as it is, at the moment she's putting everything she has into her career. It doesn't look like she'll be settling down any time soon.'

'I don't want to think about that stuff right now,' added Daffodil. She was cagey about it, her tone more than a little brusque. 'All I care about is finding a good manager and signing on for new shows!'

It wasn't her words that gave Qiao Xi pause, so much as that cold, haughty face of hers, and the flintiness with which she spoke. It made Qiao Xi wish their dinner would hurry up and finish.

'There are seven or eight TV channels and about five private companies looking to work with me, so I've told them to get in line. I'm in no hurry, I'm going to take my time.'

As she spoke, Daffodil took out a small mirror and, with the tiniest of combs, began combing her lengthy eyelashes. Fake, presumably. Qiao Xi wondered whether the girl had anything real left on her whole body. That spiel about her remaining so pure while living abroad was delusional, no doubt about it. No one on this earth escapes the filth. Lowering her double chin, she said mildly, 'We've been watching Daffodil's show, and it's a superb performance! She really brought that evil woman to life. My goodness, though, what about those internet posts...'

At this, Daffodil reddened, although only briefly. Her sweet, innocent expression returned before anyone could notice.

'Oh, you're telling me, Auntie! You recommended me for such an evil role! She'll haunt me for the rest of my life. Yesterday I was in a shop and the assistant said, "Aren't you Butterfly, from *A Passionate Woman*. Are you like that in real life?" And the way they look at me! There's nothing I can say...'

He Xiangxiang interrupted her daughter, laughing heartily, her face calm. Her eyes were on Daffodil, but she was clearly speaking for Qiao Xi's benefit. 'You should be happy! It's a sign of your success. Auntie recommended you for it to test your skills. Next time, of course she'll recommend you as leading lady – you're so beautiful, so sweet-natured. You just ask her if that isn't so?'

Qiao Xi avoided Daffodil's eyes, and their expectant, oh-so-innocent gaze. How was she supposed to respond to this? The answer was no. Inside, she was furious.

Da Geng piped up foolishly beside her, 'Of course she will! But, you know, it's sometimes better to play the bad guys. You're too young to remember, but back when we were kids, Chen Qiang played a villain in *The White-Haired Girl* and narrowly avoided being shot by soldiers in real life! He considered this a very great compliment.'

Qiao Xi set down her glass. 'I've opened the door,' she said, breezily. 'It's up to you to walk through. You don't need me anymore, Daffodil, you're all set – weren't you just saying so? They're all queuing up to work with you! It's getting late, and Da Geng here has a night shift in the cutting room ahead of him, so I think it's time for us to say our goodbyes.'

Her wording was intentionally blunt, but He Xiangxiang squared her shoulders, refusing to be cowed. Giggling, she settled the bill and then stood up. She and Daffodil bowed respectfully towards Qiao Xi, their fingers tightly linked.

'Sister, it's truly a blessing to have a daughter,' He Xiangxiang whispered into Qiao Xi's ear. 'She's such a comfort to me, like a warm padded jacket!'

As she leaned in, Qiao Xi caught a waft of her perfume. A perfume that, based on her past year of training, Qiao Xi could identify as Chanel – a world-class designer brand.

Qiao Xi grit her teeth. Pah! A warm padded jacket? More like her personal money tree. It was obvious the girl couldn't act for toffee, but still she was playing all sweet and innocent, like she was too pure of heart to go to bed with anyone. In which case: on her head be it! She was the kind to blame the toilet if she couldn't shit, or her knickers if she couldn't get her trousers open.

Qiao Xi, usually so amiable, cast that good nature to the wind. The moment she was home, she fired up her computer, put on her reading glasses, and opened Baidu. Typing in 'Daffodil' brought up no hits for people; 'Susan' generated thousands of results, although of course most of them for the wrong Susan.

After some lengthy scrolling, she came across the right one. The articles dated back a number of years, to just after Daffodil had taken second place in the Miss Asia competition, when some Hong Kong tabloids had written pieces on her. The first one ran:

'Other Woman' Susan lays on the sex appeal

If some women are destined to be 'the other woman', then Susan must count as one of the best. In the past two years, she's taken second place in both the Miss Asia beauty contest and the popular reality show, *Super Agent: The Hunt for the Nation's Best Actress*. These achievements have been plagued by scandal, but Susan has repeatedly insisted: 'I have always played by the rules and listened to the management's advice.' Here's hoping that today's viewers like girls who 'play by the rules'!

After almost six months, the *Best Actress* competition has drawn to a close. Contestants ate lizards, posed in swimsuits, fought fierce wrestling matches and, finally, the time came to announce the three champions! But rumours are circling that last-minute changes were made behind the scenes. First place was switched from Lu Ni to so-called 'pretty girl' Yao Qili, while second place went to Susan and third to Wu Kaina.

These results stirred up quite a quarrel, at the centre of which was the cruelly-ousted Lu Ni. She made a scene at the ceremony, refusing to let her erstwhile competition sister, Susan, off the hook. According to Lu Ni, Susan has a hidden nasty side, which revealed itself on the night of the finals, when she taught Lu Ni the wrong dance! Almost immediately, Little Miss Lu Ni realised the mistake, and drama ensued. And after Miss Lu's impassioned speech on the matter, it was Susan's turn to take the stage. But of course – the so-called 'other woman' has rights too, not to mention a rule-abiding good girl reputation to uphold. Let her speak!

'Other woman or not, any prize is surely better than no prize! And, honestly, we won our places fair and square. Yao Qili will sign on with Emperor Entertainment, and that's wonderful. I messed up a bit in the eighth round, I didn't act so well and I let the boss down. Qili did much better.'

'People say Qili is a dark horse, but everyone has their own definition for what that means. This is a competition, but I don't see myself as losing to her. I've also worked very hard, played by the rules and listened to the management's advice.'

Qiao Xi took off her glasses and rubbed her eyes. 'Huh,' she mused, 'I knew about Miss Asia, but I had no idea she'd been in this Best Actress thing! Seems like she didn't want to draw attention to it, otherwise why wouldn't she have told me?'

'It's time for bed!' said Da Geng. 'Stop digging around or it'll never end. So she entered a few competitions, what does it matter? You did your good deed, you're the bigger person, now just leave it be!'

Qiao Xi put her glasses back on. 'You go ahead and sleep,' she replied, not even turning to look at him. 'I want to find out what this young lady's been up to. I want to know whether she's as angelic as her mother would have us believe.'

The next news article went some way to confirming her suspicions:

Susan's nips steal the limelight at poolside show

Fourteen hopeful young actresses went on an outdoor shoot in Guangzhou's Panyu district yesterday, posing around the pool of the Chateau Star River Peninsula Hotel in ultra-skimpy bikinis. Worried the pale, flimsy swimwear would turn see-through when wet, the management forbade the girls from going in the water. To further protect their modesty, the girls were also required to tape down the edges.

Susan stuck down her bikini top, only to find it had the opposite of the desired effect: the outline of her nipples became especially prominent beneath the fabric. After the shoot, ignoring the management directives, Lu Ni and Susan started splashing about in the water with their feet, apparently unconcerned about the consequences. A representative quickly stepped in to put an end to it, leaving the two girls red-faced.

The competition for the *Best Actress* prize is fierce, and the girls' figures have noticeably 'shrunk' from how they were at the start. Lu Ni reveals that she's lost twenty pounds since she began. She was recently diagnosed with severe constipation but, with treatment, is now much better. Originally, fifteen girls were due to take part in the shoot, but Yao Qili was forced to drop out due to illness.

'Ha, "opposite of the desired effect", my foot! Of course it was deliberate! She wasn't concerned about exposing herself, she was concerned she might not. Shame those assets of hers are so small, I dare say that she could strip completely naked and they'd still be hard to spot.'

As she spoke, Qiao Xi examined the photo in question – in all honesty, none of the actresses was particularly blessed in that department.

Her son was on his way to bed and yawned as he passed behind her. 'Mum, what are you muttering on about now?'

But Qiao Xi kept on scrolling. Things were getting more and more interesting.

Eastday.com, 25th June: today marks the day of the annual Dragon Boat Festival, and three of the contestants from *Super Agent: The Hunt for the Nation's Best Actress* – Fei'er, Susan and Ouyang Yan – came out not only to eat zongzi dumplings, but also to get a taste for what it's like to be a 'human dumpling'. And there's no doubt these three human dumplings were the scrummiest of the lot.

After waging a slanging match against another contestant, Fang Ting, Fei'er has been 'on ice' all week, suspended from taking part in the show's activities. Yesterday, however, she was defrosted and posing for photos once again – and the self-declared 'spicy dumpling' was in red-hot form. Her doting management seems to have well and truly welcomed her back into the fold.

Wu Mingchang, executive producer of the show, comments on her time out: 'The two actresses involved are still very young. Their behaviour was not professional and was negatively affecting the show. We needed to discipline them, and the most straightforward way seemed to be a suspension. Fei'er was banned from attending the last dance round and Fang Ting had work, so could not fit it in either. We admonished them each individually for the incident, and they both apologised. This being the case, we decided we could fix things and there was no point in eliminating them, thereby ruining their prospects!'

On the day of the altercation, the two girls stormed out of the studio, putting their director, Liang Jilun, in a very tight spot. The management required that the two girls make public apologies to Jilun. This was intended as a warning to the other contestants, although the management also made it clear that, next time, they wouldn't be so lenient.

The three dumplings who showed up today were almost knocked out in an early round of the competition. Fei'er tried to perform a comic sketch but kept on pausing and saying, 'I can't do it...' in English, refusing to kiss Zeng Shize for the camera; she lost out for not being professional enough. In hers, Susan wouldn't act out giving birth, as her acting skills weren't up to it. And Ouyang Yan simply wasn't brave enough to go through with the lizard eating challenge. But the management let them stay on, reasoning that it was a test of endurance, and they still had time to prove themselves. To which all three girls declared: 'I will fight to the death! I will not be beaten!'

Qiao Xi cackled loudly, calling to her husband and son: 'Come over here, quick, take a look at this! A human dumpling, ready to fight to the death! Perhaps that's the truth of it. What's the saying? He who plays dirtiest, wins.'

They shuffled over, dressed in their slippers and pyjamas. Her son accidentally knocked the mouse, bringing up another article, which stunned all three of them into silence:

Best Actress contestant Susan begs management not to rule out X-rated offers

After being crowned runner-up Miss Asia, Susan returned to the limelight with a turn on *Super Agent: The Hunt for the Nation's Best Actress*, once again winning second place. In both cases, she may have been 'the other woman', but she's still signed on with Pershing, and holds out hopes of striking it big in showbiz. She's a woman on a mission, saying in no uncertain terms: 'Oh yes, I'm very ambitious, but I'm not sure what's in the store for me next. Let's see what Pershing has lined up! After watching me on *Best Actress,* they have a pretty good handle on where my strengths lie.'

Pershing is currently low on starlets, with girls hopping jobs or leaving to get married, and Susan hopes to use this to her advantage. 'I want to be their number one,' she says. 'My look is timeless, a great fit for both period and contemporary roles. I'd love to get into soaps!'

She adds: 'Since I was chosen, I've been contacted by a number of producers and adult magazines, and I just refer them all on to Pershing!'

A lot of people look down on the *Best Actress* girls, assuming that they're shameless, and destined for futures in low-rent productions – to which Susan says: 'I lived abroad for a long time, and people weren't so conservative about these things. I'll be honest, if an offer for an X-rated movie comes in, I wouldn't necessarily reject it out of hand. It would depend on the quality and the budget...'

They were silent for a while, and then Qiao Xi smacked the table. 'You see! I knew she was hiding something, behind that wooden little girl act of hers...'

Her son seemed to find her outrage entertaining. 'Karma's real, Mum! All your scheming has come back to bite you – she's playing you at your own game. She's really done a number on you, hasn't she?'

That night, Qiao Xi tossed and turned, unable to catch a wink of sleep. She kept thinking that the girl must be a truly stellar actress! She couldn't have pulled off something like this when she was that age – was this a sign of progress, or a degeneration in human nature? So thinking, she suddenly sat up and, to the background of her husband's thunderous snores, made a quiet phone call.

Six months later, on another Sunday afternoon, a substantially rounder Qiao Xi was once again sprawled out for a nap. The doorbell rang. Through the spy hole in the front door, she saw Daffodil and her mother. After hesitating for the briefest of seconds, she let them in. This time, Miss Asia sported a flowing silk mourning gown, and seemed to have reverted to her wooden beauty ways. He Xiangxiang was the same as ever, her face loaded up with smiles. This time, rather than gold bars, she had come armed with a glittering set of commemorative Olympic coins.

'Just a little visit to say hello! Don't you want to look inside the box? It's a silly souvenir, a tiny token of our appreciation... Daffodil, greet your aunt and uncle! You're a big girl now, stop acting like a bashful child.'

Keeping her expression determinedly neutral, Qiao Xi refused to meet their eyes.

'It's been months,' she said. 'Daffodil, you must be a huge star by now! Your run as Butterfly caused quite the sensation. Have you made it through your queue of adoring media people yet, and signed onto dozens of new shows?'

Daffodil pouted like a young girl and, before He Xiangxiang could open her mouth, replied, 'What new shows? I thought this was it, that things were about to take off, but I haven't signed a single contract. I'm still looking, but all I get offered are walk-on parts...'

'Why don't you leave this to me,' intercepted He Xiangxiang. 'Your aunt here has magical powers, because if it weren't for her, you could be the hottest film star in the country, and still struggle to get yourself on prime time TV...'

Inwardly, Qiao Xi scoffed, thinking, *Huh, so you did realise, after all.* But her face gave nothing away, and she answered, mildly, 'Well, of course it was Daffodil who had to put the work in, otherwise my recommendation would have been useless.'

Seeing that Qiao Xi had taken out a cigarette, He Xiangxiang rushed to light it.

'My dear,' she muttered, as she did so, 'I heard about the big feature your station's doing on the Olympics. Is it cast yet? Daffodil would be perfect for the lead role, of the girl on the diving team!'

'Well, you two are more in the know than I am. What girl on the diving team? What big feature about the Olympics? I'm not sure I know anything about this...' Qiao Xi exhaled leisurely, blowing a smoke ring, her eyes raised to the ceiling.

'Don't they mean *Wave Champion*?' piped up Da Geng. 'But the lead for that's already fixed.'

'Yes! Yes, that's the one! And if the lead's taken, well, then the number two role would also be fine. Or the third, or fourth! You have no idea just how desperate the girl is to act.'

He Xiangxiang's voice sounded choked with emotion. Tears were welling in her eyes.

'Every time, they ask her age. And we're just not willing to lie about it...and so nobody signs her. Tell us, what are we supposed to do?'

He Xiangxiang had finally worked her way through her impeccably prepared formalities and was reduced to saying what she really meant. Qiao Xi slid her eyes off the ceiling and onto her weeping cousin, quietly enjoying the spectacle. Were she to nod her head, even very slightly, she knew those tears would melt away like beeswax; she also knew that, whether she nodded or shook her head, Daffodil's fate was sealed. But the set of commemorative coins was arrayed on the table, and it was very fine indeed. Glinting in the rays of sunlight pouring through the window, it looked even shinier than last year's gold bars.

'Have a seat, let's chat.' Qiao Xi stubbed out her cigarette, and Da Geng rose to draw the curtains. In the weak evening light, she noticed a few new wrinkles on Daffodil's well-polished face.

Another dusk had fallen.

Silver Shield

Every year after the autumn harvest, Weizi village put on an opera. Feng'er started looking forward to it well in advance, counting down the days on her fingers. Elegant, reed-like fingers, that rippled up and down like piano keys.

Feng'er was fourteen. She had pale, honey-coloured skin and a waist as slender and supple as a reed bending in the wind. Her narrow eyes glistened as though perpetually brimming with tears and she wore her coppery black hair in a long plait, a seasonal flower tucked in one side. The older villagers would sigh at the sight of her, exclaiming that she was just like her mother when she was a girl.

For as long as she could remember, the only parent Feng'er had known was her dad. He was the best mat weaver in the village. His every idle moment was spent crouched on his little bamboo stool, buried in loose reeds, weaving them together. Bit by bit, snowy white mats flowed from his hands and spilled across the floor, their whiteness all the more stark against the sun-baked darkness of his skin. In Feng'er's mind, he was always weaving, and gradually that posture hardened and set, until he hunched over even when standing, appearing shorter than other people. Feng'er had never known what his eyes looked like, because they were always angled down, pupils carefully shielded by his eyelids. When she was very small, she could creep under and look up, seeing two dusky spots of light. But now, all she could see were his greying eyelashes, blinking wearily.

The stage was up. It was very big. Four carved wooden pillars rose imposingly from its floor. A gaudy wooden board had been set up beneath the village's big brass bell, displaying the names of the male and female leads. None of the villagers had any idea who they were, but this didn't stop them acting as though they did, nodding knowledgeably as they read. When the performance started, Feng'er noticed that Ah Ji was there, and that she, too, had brought along a little wooden stool to sit on. Feng'er and Ah Ji were firm friends, despite their difference in age. Ah Ji had moved to a neighbouring village after her marriage, and this was her first time back. Feng'er was thrilled, although you would never have known it – she smiled shyly, toying with Ah Ji's plait. Ah Ji had filled out a lot since she'd been gone, her breasts swelling proudly beneath her top and her new curves making the hem of her skirt look shorter. She was wearing a long red dress, in one of those loud, scarlet shades that you could spot from a hundred miles off. Her laugh was as ready as it always had been, although there was something vacant about her eyes; they didn't light up like they used to. All the other women said she was looking radiant. Only Feng'er disagreed.

Up on stage, the young actress playing the Hua Dan role warbled away for a while, and then the leading lady came out to join her. The second she appeared, Feng'er gasped in shock – this actress looked just like someone she knew, she was sure of it. She racked her brains, mentally working through every woman in the village, before finally settling on herself. That was it! The face of this Qing Yi actress was paler and a little rounder, but otherwise the two were practically identical. Feng'er looked nervously around, unsettled by the realisation, but everyone else was absorbed in the performance. Including Ah Ji.

The leading lady had a wide, fair, beautiful face. She wore a sapphire-blue robe and a pink satin waistcoat, covered in embroidery. The Qing Yi character, it was to be assumed, had spent her whole life cloistered deep in the women's quarters, where she had never laid eyes on a man. And so when she caught sight of that official's son, with his sharp little mouth and hollow, ape-like cheeks, she was shaken to the core: she drew back, her eyes wide, her whole body quivering like a leaf. The old lady of the house moved to block her view, but she stamped and craned her head to the side, acting all 'woe is me!', weeping and wailing with abandon. The girls and young women in the audience wept along with her – Feng'er stole another look at Ah Ji, and saw she was no exception. Later on, the maiden's amorous feelings subsided and she lay in bed, stricken with illness. A length of white silk put an end to her suffering, and her gentle soul wavered in the air, then departed. The next time she appeared on stage, she was shrouded in white. Her white silk noose was wound around her head, indicating that she was a spirit now. Her face was covered in chalk, her blackened eyebrows and blood-red lips startlingly prominent through the rising coils of grey smoke. The audience's tears changed to horror and alarm.

Throughout it all, Feng'er could think of only one thing: rushing backstage to find the actress after the performance. As a result, she couldn't have told you the first thing about the story line. When it was finally over, she slithered like a mudfish under the armpits of brawny audience men and their dolled-up wives, not even pausing for Ah Ji.

It was brightly decorated backstage, but there was none of the mystique Feng'er had always imagined in a place like that. The same performers who, minutes before, had been so poised and refined, striding about the stage, were now screeching and cracking raucous jokes, the air filled with their tossed off bras and underpants. Feng'er thought she recognised a slender waist above an ample backside, but a glance into the mirror revealed the owner to have a tiny, heart-shaped face. The face was freshly scrubbed of make-up and, without its dramatic eye shadow and lipstick, looked as blank as a rubber mask. It was the face of a young girl. She caught Feng'er's eye, her expression turning stern. She asked whether something was the matter. Feng'er stayed calm, covering her mouth with a hand and muttering that she'd got the wrong person, then turned away. The girl asked again, but Feng'er didn't answer. She tiptoed around and around the dressing room, where all the reflections in the mirrors looked vaguely familiar but none were the beautiful maiden.

All of a sudden, she drew up short, having run into the troupe director and his production manager. The manager moved to throw Feng'er out but was blocked by the director. This director was famous for his powers of observation and reasoned that a pretty young girl so enthralled by actors removing their make-up might be a future performer in the making.

'May I help you, young lady?' he asked softly, walking over to her.

But it was precisely this soft tone that startled Feng'er. She raised her teary eyes and said, 'Please, Mister, I'm looking for the Qing Yi actress, do you know where the Qing Yi actress has gone?'

Still optimistic about his new recruit, the director smiled widely and replied, 'What do you want with her? You'd like her to teach you to act, is that it?'

Not knowing how to answer, Feng'er nodded, and then shook her head.

'I do like her,' she said, 'that part's true. But I don't want her to teach me.'

The man stiffened.

'You'll never find her, even I don't know her full name. The second she's off stage, she grabs her money and leaves, still in all her make-up. You've no chance!'

Feng'er was stunned for a moment. 'But Mister, you could help me! Please help me, I just want to say one quick thing. I'll do anything you ask!'

The director chuckled. 'Wouldn't your parents have a thing or two to say about that, young lady? You're lucky it's me you're talking to! What if you'd got some bad fellow instead? He could have snatched you away… I'll tell you what, how about we get you in here the next time she turns up for a performance and fix you up with a nice little walk-on part? One of the children, something like that. Then you'll be able to see her, won't you?'

Feng'er hung her head and thought it over, then looked up and smiled. Her smile was like a gentle wisp of smoke. To the director, this was an unfamiliar sight; he was used to the mega-watt smiles of his actresses, blooming wide and garish as dahlia blossoms. Beautiful, but he couldn't stand how polished they were, like painted opera masks.

Something stirred in him. From inside his costume, he pulled out a silver shield.

'It's real silver,' he said. 'When you're ready to perform, hang this beneath the big bell at the entrance to the village and the woman you're looking for will appear.'

Feng'er turned the shield over in her hands. It may have been real silver, but it was also old. The images and words engraved on the front were totally foreign to her, the multi-layered design even more intricate than the most delicately woven reed mat. She could make out a western-style picture, of two men and a woman. The woman was lying on the floor, a sword through her neck, and the two men stood panic-stricken by her side. They were in a big, high-ceilinged room – a palace, by the looks of it, luxurious beyond Feng'er's wildest dreams.

By the time Feng'er was back outside, the audience had dispersed. There was only one person left, standing motionlessly under the big, starry sky. She was straight-backed, her long hair blowing about, flexing like jellyfish tentacles. It was Ah Ji.

Behind an old picture frame, Feng'er uncovered her very first secret. In those days, the contents of the frame were constantly changing. One day, it might be the painting entitled, 'Chairman Mao traverses the Motherland'; the next, it would change to, 'Chairman Mao goes to Anquan.' Feng'er was delighted to be the one who carried out these switches. But, one day, she was changing the picture over when a photo slipped from inside the frame's backing. An old, sepia photo. In it, a woman held a child. Her hair was combed into two thick plaits, and she wore a striped traditional tunic. The child was naked, staring wide-eyed at the camera. They both looked stiff and ill at ease. The woman's face was wide and fair and beautiful, although also slightly foolish; you could see instantly that she was nervous, unused to posing in photo studios for portraits.

Feng'er pored over the photo, then stuck it up beside her reflection in the mirror. She was convinced that there was a resemblance between her and the woman, and she stared at the sepia image so intently that it seemed to float off the page. Or, to be more precise: the woman seemed to float off the page. And as she did so, her shape morphed and grew, as though someone were steadily enlarging the photo. Before Feng'er had time to be afraid, the photo had grown to ten times its original size, and she could make out a flicker of a smile playing at the corners of the woman's mouth. Then she heard a voice, drifting in mid-air. It was very faint, and she heard only, 'Reed', followed by some other word she couldn't quite make out. Then the mirror went blank.

As soon as she heard Feng'er was sick, Ah Ji asked her husband for half a day off, saying that she was going to Weizi village to buy a couple of mats. Before leaving, she went to fill a bottle with some of Feng'er's favourite glutinous rice wine, sweet as honey and made with her own fair hands. Her mother-in-law heard her come in to decant it and grunted from behind her mosquito net, 'I love that rice wine, don't you go touching it!'

Ah Ji told her to go back to sleep, reassuring her that she was doing no such thing. The old lady rolled over and nodded off again. Ah Ji then poured out a large helping, replacing it with a generous dollop of cold water. She put back the original container and slipped the bottle for Feng'er into her bosom. As she did so, her mind raced with angry thoughts: *You nosy old busybody, anyone would think you never ate a decent meal in your life! Even if you don't care about me, what about the precious Liang family line – don't you care about your grandson? You're practically dead, and here you are fighting him for food!*

Ah Ji donned her bamboo sunhat and left, at which the old lady rose from her feigned slumber to watch through the window lattice, her mind also buzzing with anger: *It's the middle of autumn, what does she need a sun hat for! She's not some blushing maiden anymore, what's she going round trying to look pretty for? Who cares if her belly's swelling! Whose hasn't, at one time or another…* Ah Ji's mother-in-law had been widowed as a young woman, leaving her to raise her son alone. She couldn't bear to witness any sign of affection between the couple.

As she approached Feng'er's house, Ah Ji heard music. A wretched, mournful tune, like someone sobbing. As usual, Feng'er's dad was by the front door, far too engrossed in his weaving to look up and greet a visitor.

'Where's Feng'er?' asked Ah Ji.

Feng'er's dad twitched his mouth towards the house. This was how it had always gone, whenever Ah Ji used to visit; it felt like stepping back in time, to before she was married. To when the reed pond was jade-green and Feng'er wore a hibiscus in her hair. Ah Ji remembered Feng'er feeding her a big handful of elm pods, and how the pods had been infused with the sweet scent of her hands. Back then, Ah Ji was embroidering headdresses to save up for her dowry, finishing a new one every day.

Feng'er was playing her *xiao*. People said she was lucky. With a dad as capable as hers, she had time to play that bamboo flute and sketch sewing patterns; to perfect the feminine arts. Feng'er carried on playing, even after Ah Ji had entered – this was her way, and Ah Ji didn't mind it. She simply set the bottle of rice wine to one side and listened quietly.

The sun in autumn was less fierce than in the summer, but still it made people lazy. While listening to the music, Ah Ji's thoughts turned to that starry night after the opera. She had waited a long time. When Feng'er finally appeared, her eyes were glistening. She seemed excited. 'Ah Ji,' she said, 'let's go to the reed pond! It must be ages since you went.'

And so the two of them linked arms and walked over to the reed pond. The moon was bright and there was a gentle breeze. Ah Ji told Feng'er that she was pregnant. Feng'er did not seem surprised. 'Do you want a boy or a girl?' she asked, although she seemed distracted. And Ah Ji's response was even stranger than Feng'er's disinterest.

'Neither,' she said. 'Once she has a baby, a woman's life is over. Feng'er, remember that time we were bathing in the reed pond, and you said my waist was so slim you could wrap your hand around it? Well, now look at me—'

Ah Ji had always been impatient, and when Feng'er failed to respond, she lifted her clothes to show her. Feng'er saw that Ah Ji's slender waist had vanished, and her once lovely little breasts were now so swollen that all the veins were visible. Her nipples had turned dark, and a livid stretchmark ran right around her waist; Feng'er imagined a blood-sucking tapeworm gestating behind the taut skin. But Ah Ji's face was still the same, even if her body was no longer her own. With a tight little laugh, she said, 'Ever noticed how pregnant women look like cows? And this is just the beginning. Wait until the thing's born, then it'll drink all my milk and I'll get fat as a barrel. Soon enough, my flesh will go slack and droopy, like a sow's belly, and I'll disgust anyone who lays eyes on me. I'll be skinny again in time to die, and that's how all of us so-called fairer sex end up: skeletons, the lot of us.'

In the moonlight, Feng'er's face looked as pale as starch jelly.

'Does it have to be that way for every woman?' she asked.

Ah Ji gave another of her laughs. 'No, some women do it differently. You remember Auntie Liu, that old lady from one village over, who's gone her whole life without a man? Look how it turned out for her.

Even worse than for a married woman, don't you think? Once I passed her in the village, and I knew I should say something, to be respectful to my elders. So I said, "How do you do" and she spun around, her eyes boring right into me, and said, "What the hell do you want?" I nearly jumped out of my skin. I heard she had breast cancer a couple of years ago, but they found it early and operated, only now it's come back in her womb. You know why? Because she never married, never had children, and so her blood got blocked. Of course she got cancer!'

Feng'er was crouched on the ground. 'So you're saying that whatever a woman does, it's no good?' she said. 'I don't want to get fat and obviously I don't want to get cancer, so maybe I'll just die at nineteen. I won't live a day longer than that! On my nineteenth birthday, I'll drown myself in this pond!'

Ah Ji cut her off, covering Feng'er's mouth with her hands.

'Don't be silly! No matter what, it's better to be alive than dead. And, listen, some women are special. Some women live full and happy lives and don't ever get old. They're beautiful right up until the day they die. Like your mother, she was one of those. One in a million. It's such a tragedy that she was taken from us so soon...'

Before Ah Ji could finish, there came a sudden gust of wind. It's true: at exactly that point in their conversation, a gust of wind. The reeds in the pond surged like a tide and dark grey clouds whipped along the horizon. There was a sound like someone sobbing, or like the weepy tones of a *xiao*; a misery that struck right at the hearts of the two young women.

They had very different memories of what happened next. Ah Ji remembered pulling Feng'er up and running for shelter, heading for the nearest hut they could find. According to Ah Ji, Feng'er was panting, her face drained of all colour, and she asked, 'Ah Ji, did you see the boat? There's a boat on the pond!' Ah Ji said she must be crazy, no one round there would ever dare go out on the reed pond in the dark, let alone with the weather like that! Feng'er corrected herself: there wasn't a person on the boat, the boat was sailing itself! That's right, according to Feng'er, there was no mistaking it. Behind a patch of reeds blown flat by the wind, she quite clearly saw a boat sailing towards them from the horizon. It cast an enormous shadow across the glimmering surface of the water.

In years to come, the image would remain sharp in Feng'er's mind. When she thought back to that night, she would think of the dark wind stirring through the dark expanse of reeds, of a mysterious little boat sailing silently through the night, of the little boat's enormous dark shadow.

Feng'er channeled that wind into her music. Ah Ji could detect it, although she couldn't understand why Feng'er would want to preserve such a memory.

At long last, Feng'er put down her flute. 'Ah Ji,' she said, smiling weakly, 'would you do me a favour?'

Ah Ji asked what it was and then told her to cheer up, no need to get all serious and pedantic about it. Feng'er opened a case and took out the silver shield. Ah Ji examined it but couldn't make head or tail of the delicate engravings.

'Was it your Ma's?' she asked. Feng'er shushed her, shaking her finger, and Ah Ji understood that she didn't want her dad to hear.

'It doesn't matter where I got it,' said Feng'er. 'On your way home, I need you to hang it underneath the big bell at the entrance to the village, okay?'

Ah Ji stared at her in shock. 'But sweetie, why?'

Feng'er told her not to ask questions. In a few days, all would be revealed.

On her way out, Ah Ji noticed that Feng'er's father was more hunched than ever. It seemed that the music really had channelled the wind, blowing so that he was bent double. He was shivering with cold.

It was very late when he finally came inside. Instead of turning on the light, he lit a candle, but the flame went out almost instantly.

Someone was standing behind him.

'Dad,' she said, 'how did Ma die?'

Her voice was low, but he started to shake violently; it was the shaking that put out the flame. He hadn't expected his daughter would be awake.

Feng'er watched her father's trembling hunch. Without turning to face her, he replied, 'How did she die? Didn't I tell you? She drowned in the reed pond.'

'But how?'

'Ah, your mother was a stubborn one. The unit secretary said she hadn't woven enough mats, so she went out that night to cut reeds to make more...'

'How come we don't have any pictures of her?'

'We were very poor back then, barely had enough to eat. What would we be spending money on photos for?'

'Well, who's that woman in the photo behind the Chairman Mao poster, then?'

Feng'er's eyes sliced into his back like swords. His body went limp as a pile of rags.

'You've been lying to me all along,' said Feng'er, crying now. 'I'm fourteen years old and you still won't tell me the truth!'

Then she ran out of the room, without any idea where she was running to.

Ah Ji grasped the shield in both hands, examining it as she walked. It was only at night that the tarnished silver surface gleamed slightly. Its mysterious engravings made Ah Ji imagine a murder case in some far-off country – the powers of her imagination extended only so far as plot lines she'd seen on television. She had a very good television set at home. She thought of one show in particular: two men were in love with the same woman. One of them married her; let's call him Man X. One day, Man X went away on a trip, and Man Y – the other one – came over to the house to reminisce with the woman about their former affections. Naturally, this caused a resurgence in these former affections, and they ended up spending the night together. X returned to discover the scene, and ended up in a sword fight with Y. After several rounds, they still couldn't determine a winner, and so X turned to the woman and said, 'You be the judge. Only one of us shall remain.' The woman burst into noisy sobs, then picked up a sword and pointed it at herself. After she collapsed in a pool of blood, Man Y quickly slipped away – at which point, the woman rose from the puddle and revealed it all to have been a trick. The blood had come from a bag of chicken blood that she had concealed under her clothes. And so, in the end, the woman and her husband lived happily ever after.

The scene on the shield depicted the exact moment that the woman had fallen, clutching the sword. But Ah Ji was not about to leave things at that. Noticing an uneven patch on the back, she felt about until her fingers settled on a tiny drawer. She gently tugged it open and a scrap of white fabric fluttered out, with some kind of symbol painted on it. Before she could get a grip, it flew out of her fingers, flapping like a live thing, rising into the night sky like a spirit.

Feng'er saw the shield hanging beneath the bell at the entrance to the village. In the moonlight, it took on a coppery sheen. The moon that night was pink, hanging high in the sky, like a midnight sun. Feng'er stood uncertainly beneath it, until at long last she heard a distant commotion. Another big stage had been erected. She could faintly make out the shapes of villagers crowded around it. They must really be crazy about opera, she thought to herself; the bell hadn't even sounded, and still they knew it was time. And then it struck her: could this be because of the shield? She looked over at it, and it was hanging there just as before. No one had touched it.

The Hua Dan girl came onto the stage, yipping and ya-ing, decked out in purple brocade and a beaded headdress. After her song, she pressed her fingers into the lotus position, waiting for someone. She was the same actress as last time, and Feng'er assumed she must be waiting for the Qing Yi actress from before. She craned her neck to see but, when the Qing Yi character appeared, she was played by the girl with the heart-shaped face. Flustered, Feng'er hurried for the backstage, squeezing under the armpits of the crowd.

Backstage was still a riot of colour. The troupe director raised his head from inside a suit of armour, seemingly not at all surprised to see Feng'er. She asked him why the actress had changed, and he said, 'What do you mean changed? It's always been the same girl.'

'No,' said Feng'er, feeling a jolt of panic. 'No, last time it was a woman with a beautiful round face! She looked nothing like the one tonight.'

The director chuckled and said, 'Well, child, you must have been dreaming. Ask anyone you like.'

So saying, he collared a clown that was just about to head onto the stage. The clown wrinkled his white-powdered nose, and said there'd only ever been one Qing Yi actress, ever since the troupe began, and it was that girl on the stage with the heart-shaped face.

Feng'er was stunned. She wondered whether she was dreaming, but it hurt when she pinched her face. Why would the director say such a thing? Were they all conspiring against her? Perhaps they thought this was funny. She turned to the director, her eyes brimming with tears.

'Mister, last time I was here you gave me a silver shield. You said I just had to hang it up and the Qing Yi lady would appear. Don't tell me you've forgotten? You can't deny it, Mister, the proof is right there.' She promptly dragged him out to the bell. 'You see! There it is, the silver shield is....' Feng'er suddenly stopped. Somehow, the silver shield had disappeared.

Feng'er's dad was calling for her, his creaky old voice echoing through the night.

Feng'er's dad was walking towards her, his hunched back and stumbling gait calling to mind a sick, elderly camel.

Feng'er's dad was drawing closer, and as he did so, a slip of white flickered into view.

Feng'er's dad followed that slip of white all the way to the edge of the reed pond. At the sight of the pond, his whole body began to tremble violently. It had been a good thirteen years since he'd come so close. He wove reeds into mats, but never cut the reeds himself; he had some young village boys from the village do that for him. The white slip settled on the ground and he picked it up, noticing that it contained a line of writing. He called out in a panic, shouting for Feng'er.

A boat drifted silently from among the reeds. The serene blue moon had been shining for thirteen years; it shone now just as it had back then. But thirteen years before, there had been a person on that boat. A woman with a wide, fair, beautiful face. She had been married to him for over three years, and they had a baby who had just turned one. This wife of his had never loved him. He knew that but tried not to mind. Beautiful women were proud, he thought to himself; he would work like a dog for as long as he lived, and he would do it all for her. Slow and steady wins the race. Tiny drops of water eventually grow into stalactites, and he refused to believe that he couldn't win her over eventually. So long as she was faithful, his patience knew no bounds. But then he discovered that she was not. She was always going out to cut reeds, and one day he saw her with his own eyes, out there with another man – the director of an opera troupe. He felt his heart shatter, all his blood gurgling out. He slept out there, using his reed chopper as a pillow.

In the end he did not use it against his wife. He tried as hard as he could, but there was a silver shield standing in his way. And then, all of a sudden, from deep among the reeds, a man appeared. Feng'er's father turned away from his wife, focusing instead on the man, but once again the silver shield was there, obstructing him. In all the intervening years, he had never once caught a proper glimpse of the man's face. In a rage, he overturned the little boat, right where the silt of the pond was at its deepest. The woman was sucked straight in. He had never forgotten the smile on her face in those final moments. A distant, beautiful smile. Fleeting, untouchable. Like a young girl thinking of her lover, recalling something especially charming about him. A protective, adoring expression.

The man with the shield did not rush to save her. He sprinted away. For some time, Feng'er's dad had stood rooted to the spot, before launching himself into the marshy edge of the pond like a man possessed, raking through the mud. He never found her body. What a tragedy, he thought, for the man she loved to have abandoned her like this, at the moment it mattered most. Now, thirteen years later, he watched the boat drift towards him, frosty-blue in the moonlight.

Five years later, on her nineteenth birthday, Feng'er was married. Ah Ji acted as her matchmaker. As Feng'er was an orphan, all the older village folk put in an appearance and the wedding was a lively affair. Only Ah Ji seemed troubled, refusing to leave Feng'er's side. By evening, noticing that her groom was anxious for them to be alone, Feng'er had no choice but to say something. 'Ah Ji my dear, is something the matter?' she asked.

Ah Ji hemmed and hawed, finally mumbling, 'I'm more worried something might be the matter with you. With both your parents gone, who's left to take care of you?'

Feng'er rolled her eyes. 'Ah Ji, you're worrying about that silly joke I made all those years ago, aren't you? Please don't, I'm now firmly of the opinion that even the worst life is better than a good death – and anyone who thinks otherwise is a fool! This is how it goes, isn't it? Maidens become wives, wives become mothers, and each step has its own pleasures. I intend to live a long and happy life!'

And so, not without some hesitation, Ah Ji left them be. The night passed without any disaster, and so it went: day after day, year after year, Feng'er lived a perfectly happy life. Except for one thing: she never watched another opera. When she was sad, she played her *xiao*, her music mournful, like someone sobbing. Whenever she heard it, Ah Ji thought back to the wind on that night down by the reeds, and how it had made them surge like a tide.

Marrying Out

As Qiao entered the yard, she found her way blocked by two hefty, pendulous luffa gourds. The plants were very, very old, their trailing stems and the dark brown gourd skins so cracked that they looked as though they might fall to pieces if you touched them. Grey desiccated flesh was visible through the cracks, and they were enveloped, and anchored in place, with dust and cobwebs. The smell of rot wafted from them and permeated the air. When she looked carefully, she saw that the whole yard was covered in the slimy stems, each one home to half a dozen bugs and pupae, their hard cases the size of sour dates. A plump black bird sat on the steps pecking at something. It made no effort to fly away when it saw Yuanzhi.

'Is it a raven…?' Qiao asked, somehow fearful.

'That's right, it's my great-grandmother's pet, completely tame,' said Yuanzhi with some pride. 'Taipo tames all sorts of creatures, she never kills living things!'

'Oh!'

'We've got a big black carp, she tamed that too, it's huge…' Yuanzhi sketched its size with his hands. 'Taipo's promised we can eat it at my wedding feast!'

'Oh!'

'She's looked after that fish for more than twenty years! Ever since I can remember.' Yuanzhi deftly avoided a dangling bug. 'Everyone says we're keeping a fish spirit!'

'Oh.' Qiao was following cautiously behind, occasionally bending or ducking, but still feeling the sticky stems catching at her, making her itch unbearably.

'Don't forget to greet her properly when you see her,' admonished Yuanzhi, 'the way I greeted your mum and dad!'

Qiao prodded one of the pupae, and a greenish-yellow liquid oozed out, but it did not smell bad at all. She ran her hand over a tree trunk and it came away covered with small black bugs. 'These long threads, are they all bug spit?' she asked.

Everything in the house was very old. The metal fittings were rusty, and the floor was so grey with dust, you could not see what the original colour was. When Qiao looked carefully, she realized it was crawling with ant-like creatures. The marriage bed was ready, the bedding looking celebratory in reds and greens. Qiao sneaked a look at herself in the mirror as she passed by and was pleased with her appearance. As she gave her hair a customary pat, she bumped into something, but before she had time to figure out what it was, she heard footsteps. A sort of shuffling, mixed with a tap-tapping, and the floor creaked and groaned.

'Ai-yaya! You're here!' she heard and her mother-in-law, Popo, appeared, waving long arms in welcome. She seemed light as a feather, and the ample sleeves of her black woolen sweater danced gracefully in the air like wings. She had small triangular eyes, buried deep in dark-ringed sockets, in contrast to which her nose and mouth were startlingly big (Qiao remembered her mother telling her that a big mouth was a sign of good fortune). She also had a huge wart beside one nostril (there must be a story behind that too), and when she smiled, her cheeks formed fleshy mounds and you could see two rows of strong pointed teeth. Her legs and arms were very long and thin, and she seemed to be knock-kneed. Qiao suddenly wished she could hide her own straight limbs.

But there was no hiding. Qiao felt the woman's piercing eyes on her.

She opened her mouth wide but no sound came out. She looked up but only as far as her mother-in-law's chest, which was oddly flat. She made a hurried bow, drawing in her own high-set breasts. Her father-in-law, Gonggong was standing firmly apart from his wife, Qiao and Yuanzhi. The man had a great bull neck, and his face was florid, even verging on purple at his forehead. Even so, she could see he must have been good-looking when he was younger. He had a habit of clearing his throat then ejecting gobs of white spittle.

Yuanzhi was making a show of leafing through the calendar pages, all the while watching Qiao out of the corner of his eye. Qiao opened her mouth again but still no sound came out. Yuanzhi's beady black eyes widened. Popo quickly put in: 'You should go and see your Taipo before you do anything else.' Qiao shut her mouth and smiled at her parents-in-law, putting on a show of enjoying herself. They smiled back. Qiao looked into Popo's smiling face feeling touched, but her mother-in-law's gaze was somewhere over the top of Qiao's head, despite all Qiao's efforts to catch her eye. Popo shut her mouth, no doubt feeling she had smiled enough. The huge wart by her nose caught the light and jerked as her face moved. A finger on Qiao's right hand suddenly jerked in response.

'Get her to tidy her hair!' Popo said with a snort, and Yuanzhi hurriedly turned to neaten Qiao's mussed-up hair.

It was dim in the inner room, with a thick curtain at the window, and something smelled rotten to Qiao. This room must be where the fermenting cabbage was kept. On Taipo's bed, the coverlet was laid out and part of a steaming hot water bottle was visible. A moist smell of plaster rose from the bedding.

A loud fart came from the kitchen. Popo laughed: 'The old lady must be hungry!' Popo had long flat buttocks. Qiao suddenly remembered reading in a weird book that the parts of the body had a mysterious way of growing alike, so she guessed that Popo's breasts were as long and pendulous as her buttocks, probably reaching right down to her navel. She felt sorry for Gonggong. This was probably the only woman he had ever seen naked in his life.

Taipo was busy ladling something from an old-fashioned clay pot that was thickly covered in grease. A warm ray of sunlight shone in and Qiao saw the air was filled with flying insects, hovering like dust motes. A large pork elbow was stewing in the pot, a layer of oil concealing the broth underneath. Someone had already cut off a large chunk of the meat. Taipo pursed her lips and sipped at the mush. At every sip, her iron-grey gums turned dark purple. The thick gravy dripped from her teeth, not onto her chest, but onto the floor by her feet – an oily puddle had formed and a swarm of bugs were slurping greedily. They were so fat they could barely fly. Taipo smacked her lips with relish and let out a stream of angry-sounding farts.

'Such a lot of bugs!' Qiao exclaimed. She was almost gagging, and it was hard to avoid stepping on them every time you put your foot down.

Taipo gave her a sudden poke, leaving five greasy fingerprints on her pretty, checked jumper, and wailed pitifully:

'What a sinful thing to say! What harm have they ever done you? Why would you want to kill them? They're living creatures!' Qiao suddenly felt very small. She wished she could disappear completely behind Yuanzhi.

Taipo and Popo were very alike. Both had small, triangular-shaped eyes and large triangular-shaped mouths. Taipo must originally have had a full set of pointed teeth too. But now all that was left were bare gums. It was like watching a roller at work when they opened and closed their mouths, quite impressive. They even had similar clothes, with Popo wearing a baggy black sweater and Taipo a loose unlined black jacket. Qiao wondered why they were both so keen on black, especially today, a day of celebration.

'Yuanzhi, have you got cloth ears? I told you both to get her hair sorted – you'll bring bad luck on the wedding!' Popo's eyes were so buried in dark-ringed sockets that the only gleam came from her caustic smile, and that felt like a stab from an awl. Her chest was so flat that Qiao had the impression she had no breasts at all.

Yuanzhi looked blank, as if he had not heard his mother's instruction, then quickly gave a bright smile in case people should think he was half-witted. 'Dad, will we be getting the wedding photo enlarged?' he said inconsequentially.

'Go…g-g-go.. and t-t-talk to your m-m-m-mother!' Gonggong replied, deferring to his wife. In spite of his stammer, however, he had a good voice, with precise, articulate delivery.

'Mother, for the photo in our wedding outfit, I found this flower, it's the only pink one I could find, the others are all red.' Qiao was trying hard to make a good impression on Popo.

'Very good! You'll be blessed!' said Popo, but her tones felt to Qiao like a desiccated broom that was sweeping her heart out, leaving it desolate and empty.

Taipo gave Qiao a patting-down all over with her greasy hands, and huffed and puffed: 'Such a titchy pelvis, how're you going to get babies out of there?' Popo pursed her lips, and looked a little embarrassed, then suddenly rolled her trouser legs all the way up to the top of her thighs. As Qiao looked on in astonishment, she calmly hopped into a big wooden tub with clothes soaking in it, and commenced to tread them vigorously, sending splashes of white foam flying and revealing the sallow skinny legs that Qiao had imagined. She really was knock-kneed. Popo trod so briskly that she made a long vein in each calf jiggle.

'Mother, let me do that…' Qiao began, feeling that she ought to play the good daughter-in-law, but Popo took no notice at all, just carried on cheerfully treading. A while later, however, she actually turned bashful: Gonggong was talking to her and his voice was full of warmth. Perhaps this wedding day was their only chance to be flirtatious with each other, perhaps those stumpy knock-kneed legs held a special place in Gonggong's affections. Qiao felt she had misjudged them.

What should I do? What should we do? Qiao looked her questions at Yuanzhi, but Yuanzhi was doing his best to avoid her eyes. They were both covered in bug spittle, despite the fact that they had been so careful walking through the yard. And it was horribly itchy.

'Come on, time for a game of mahjong!' Taipo was shouting at them. Yuanzhi pushed in front of Qiao, nearly knocking her over, and fled into the back room. What on earth had scared Yuanzhi? Qiao wondered.

'When you play mahjong with Taipo, you can't win all the time, or lose all the time either,' Yuanzhi was instructing her in a whisper now. Yuanzhi lost the draw and invited Taipo to lead, putting on a mischievous air. Taipo responded by putting out a stick-like hand to pat his mustachioed face affectionately. Qiao smiled too, but inwardly felt embarrassed. There was another rattle of farts from Taipo and Yuanzhi cried: 'Pay no attention! Taipo's so blessedly healthy! Is it any wonder that you're still going strong at eighty-eight?! Your good health is heaven-sent!' Then Qiao forgot Yuanzhi's injunctions and played a winning hand. Taipo fell grimly silent. Then there was another loud report. Qiao was so startled she did not know where to look.

'Granny, you're an old lady, you've probably got a bit of indigestion,' she said tremulously.

'Who says? Farts are our *qi*, and they're better out than in!' Yuanzhi exclaimed, gesticulating vigorously. 'Especially Taipo's farts, they're not ordinary *qi*, they're magic!' He got another affectionate pat on the face from Taipo and, by way of reward, she fished a morsel of pork out of her bowl for him. It was not properly cooked. (For some odd reason, Taipo liked it like that.) Yuanzhi pretended it was delicious and passed it to Qiao. Qiao took a nibble and a bad smell filled her nostrils. She rushed to the bathroom and threw up. She retched and retched and wished she never had to come out. It seemed to her that the bathroom was the only clean place in the house. She was just admiring the gleaming white porcelain toilet when Yuanzhi rushed in and threw up a bloody piece of meat. Qiao retched again, and they vomited in unison.

As they came out, they heard something banging around in the bathtub. Taipo had jumbled up all the mahjong pieces and was squinting and laughing at them. Popo was laughing too. She had rolled her trouser legs down, and the clothes were washed. Gonggong laughed along with his wife and mother. He had a loud laugh, like a horse's neigh. It seemed to give Popo a fright – she turned to look at him and Gonggong fell silent. Then Popo said she was going to give Gonggong a back massage and they shut themselves in their room.

Taipo was shouting that she was hungry. Yuanzhi, flushed with excitement, gesticulated at the shut door. Qiao pretended not to see and took refuge in the bathroom where she sat down on the toilet seat and was content to daydream. This time she did not forget to bolt the door. There was a small round mirror, all the mercury scratched off around the edges, only a small patch in the middle reflecting back at her. Qiao could see that the greyish mucus was beginning to form a layer of skin. Translucent, scabby skin. It began at her collarbone. She tried to scrape it off, scraped and scraped until she was trembling with pain and had scraped herself raw. The 'skin' had stuck fast to her flesh. 'Better wash it off, let's try and wash it off,' she said to herself and she stripped and jumped into the bathtub, making the carp flap around in the murky water. So that was the source of the banging! The carp floated motionless for a moment, its beady eyes scrutinizing her, then there was a flash of green and it began to leap crazily in the water, its smooth tail lashing out at her fiercely. She felt a stinging pain all over, and realized that the carp was armed with strong pointy little teeth that glinted faintly in the gloom.

Then Popo was there, her ruddy face wreathed in smiles, pinning Qiao's right hand to the edge of the tub. The big carp had been resting on the bottom, but when it heard Popo's footsteps, it leapt and splashed again, lashing out with its tail. Its eyes gleamed a sinister green. Popo laughed out loud: 'Lively critter, isn't it?! In a little while, you can kill it for dinner and pick some vegetables, and we'll have a celebratory dinner!' Qiao looked at Popo and nodded. She really wanted to shake her head but something made her afraid, overcoming even her fear of the carp. So she nodded and nodded and by the time she stopped nodding, felt she had fallen into a deep pit. The fingers of her right hand, the ones so warmly gripped by Popo, began to jitter uncontrollably.

Yuanzhi and Qiao caught the carp together. Twice, as they stirred up the cloudy water, her fingers touched something slimy. She broke out into a cold sweat. The enormous fish was flapping frenziedly, and the normally mild-mannered Yuanzhi acted exasperated, though Qiao had the distinct feeling he was really terrified. By this time, they were splashed from head to foot with muddy water. Yuanzhi was red-eyed and Qiao saw he had a knife in his hand. His eyes bulged and he fixed the fish with a murderous glare. Qiao began to inch backwards. Yuanzhi was brandishing his weapon, his eyes flashing. Qiao slumped on the toilet seat. Green blood spurted out, staining the cloudy water.

The bleeding carp leapt high out of the water and hurled itself at Yuanzhi, baring its pointy venomous teeth. Its scales gleamed a lurid silvery purple, and its body twisted in the air like a python, its translucent black fins jerking back and forth demonically. Yuanzhi yelled and dropped the knife; the carp grabbed it between the teeth and kept on slithering towards him. Qiao frantically launched herself at it, and the green blood turned into a rivulet. Taipo stood amid a pile of bone fragments contentedly scraping food fragments from between her teeth.

'I've been poisoned…poisoned!' Bright green sweat was beading on Yuanzhi's forehead, and he was shivering. He raised his arms aloft. They were covered in a garish mixture of green and red blood and purple scales.

The fish landed at Popo's feet. 'Mother, it's bitten him!' Qiao was ashen-faced and could hardly get the words out. She could see the new skin thickening on her body and scabbing over, so hard that she could no longer bend forward. 'You're both completely useless! Can't you even kill a fish?' Popo glared at Qiao. And Qiao did indeed feel she was useless. Her head suddenly dropped as if it was trying to retreat into her chest and her hearing became extremely acute, as if her ears had turned into antennae. Every word her mother-in-law spoke caused her terrible pain. She watched dully as Popo reached out a misshapen, felt-slipper-clad foot (as a child, her feet had been bound but were unbound now). She stepped calmly and fearlessly on the fish's head, then twisted it to one side, shattering the bones with a crunch. The fish lay still, its pink gills flapping, eyes bulging, mouth agape, but at least those triangular teeth were no longer visible. Qiao thought that was odd. Trembling, she began to scrape the scales off and they fluttered to the ground, glinting as murderously as sword blades. When it came time to cut the fins off, the great black creature stirred. Qiao dug out the entrails with her eyes tight shut, catching a strong whiff of fermenting wine lees. When she opened her eyes again, she saw the guts had been stained green by the carp's blood. The intestinal cavity was full of seeds. Such a big fat fish and there was just a bag of seeds, no flesh at all. She was very disappointed. She cut off the cheeks, leaving its green eyeballs hanging by a thread. They fixed her with a sinister stare.

When they went to bed, Qiao felt strange. She asked Yuanzhi to check her over, but he made out it was nothing. His hands were bandaged with gauze through which seeped red and green blood. Still, he was in a state of high excitement. He rolled back and forth in bed, trying to pin her down, but she was even more difficult to deal with than the fish. His face fell. Next door, Qiao heard her mother-in-law's bed creak.

'Did you hear something?' she asked.

'Hear what?'

Qiao fell silent. She listened intently, as if her ears were on stalks. Yuanzhi listened too but heard nothing.

Qiao felt sudden cramps in her belly, but it didn't stop Yuanzhi humping her in the marriage bed – he was an uncomplicated guy, after all. Afterwards they both fell into a deep sleep. Qiao dreamt that someone was stabbing her with a knife.

She cried out in pain in her sleep and rolled all over the bed. In the midst of all the fuss she was making, she heard more creaking from the bed in the room next door. Now Yuanzhi was awake too, and also complaining of stomach pain.

'Do you think it was the fish…?' she asked, her voice trembling with fear. She saw her own panic reflected in his panic-stricken eyes.

'Popo…. Served me a big helping and I didn't dare refuse…'

'Hush!' In the darkness, the pair stared at each other, their fear mingled with hostility, as if the other was actually the great black carp.

'Its blood….was green!…'

'It must have been poisonous…!'

'It can't have been a real fish!'

'What?!' Yuanzhi shivered.

'How could a fish have teeth like that? That's why I think it wasn't a fish…'

'So what was it, then?'

They stared at each other again, in the darkness.

'Did you see its scales?…'

'Scales? No, I didn't. Scales…'

Both covered in sweat, they settled back down to sleep. Qiao had a vague sensation of something moving in her hair, and when she put her hand up to feel, she found a squashed bug, its stickiness matting several strands of hair together. No wonder Popo had said her hair was a mess, she thought. Next door, the creaking of the bed continued.

Eventually the creaking stopped. Outside, a woodpecker was tapping the trunk of an old tree. Rat-a-tat-tat, the noise came again. Qiao covered her ears, not sure whether she was awake or asleep. The noise got louder until it sounded like drumming on hollow, rotten wood. The noise penetrated deep into her brain, painfully loud. She forced her eyes open a crack. It was still dark outside but the frenzied knocking continued and the door was beginning to rock dangerously on its hinges.

'Yuanzhi! Yuanzhi! Open the door!…'

It was Popo! Qiao and Yuanzhi flung on some clothes. Yuanzhi went to open the door, his eyes still shut, forgetting that Qiao was still in her underwear. The door burst open, and Qiao froze, somehow unable to make her hands do her buttons up. She felt Popo looking daggers at her, savagely sweeping over her full bosom clad only in a vest. She saw a bulky shadow flit past the doorway outside.

'Do you know what the time is? Why aren't you up yet? Taipo's waiting for her grandson's wife to make her breakfast!' Popo said. She was looking wan and drawn, as if she had not slept a wink all night. Her face was like wax, the skin around her eyes sagged heavily and her beady gaze was filled with an enmity that Qiao would never forget. She trembled inwardly, though she did not know why. Gonggong's smile was gone too, he just kept ejecting gobs of spittle, on which small flying insects instantly settled. Taipo sat in her room with a face like thunder, impatiently tapping the side of her rice bowl. No one looked directly at her, but Qiao felt their eyes on her all the same. She felt as if she had been stripped naked. Under their venomous gaze, she needed to get dressed properly but everything felt wrong; the 'skin' she had acquired yesterday was getting thicker by the minute, covering her like a shell. She remembered the pupae hanging from the vines in the yard and was seized with panic.

'Have I…have I changed?' she asked Yuanzhi again, increasingly filled with dread. 'No… no, you haven't…' Yuanzhi was still half-asleep. All of a sudden, Qiao saw that Yuanzhi's skin was a grey colour, and covered in long smooth hairs so thick you could only see the skin beneath if you looked closely. His mouth protruded somewhat. He had gingery whiskers and wide gaps between his teeth, and round jug ears.

'Mouse!' Qiao cried. Yuanzhi's beady little eyes flew open and he started crawling around on the floor: 'Where? Where?'

Qiao stared. But Yuanzhi was still himself, with his small head and jug ears. Not handsome but good-hearted. Her mother had always said a man like this made a reliable husband.

'According to our village customs, you're a newly-married woman from the day after the wedding! You're not a guest anymore!' Popo told her. The three old folks ate their breakfast sat around three sides of the table, which was pushed against the wall. The young couple sat opposite them, on the edge of the bed. Popo got out the traditional red envelopes and gave them one each. As her wide sleeves flapped, it reminded Qiao of the black bird she had seen in the yard outside when she arrived. 'These are for luck!' Popo announced. 'You're one of us now, and this is money in advance. By this time next year, we expect to be nursing our grandson, just you remember that!' Qiao was just about to nod obediently, when a terrible smell from Taipo reached her nostrils, and she had to make a mad dash for the toilet.

The hand mirror in the bathroom was unmistakable proof that her body was now covered with a translucent shell. The nerves, veins and arteries could still be seen quite clearly beneath it, but her neck and limbs had retracted inside and it was clear that a little horn was growing from the top of her head. She felt it – it was soft, like a coxcomb. She craned her neck then retracted it again; it felt as elastic as a rubber band. She did it again. It felt funny. Was she a snail? Well, that wasn't a bad thing. She even felt pleased with herself: she was able to see things that other people couldn't see. Her eyes were different from other eyes. To others, she looked just the same, but she had grown a suit of armour. Inexplicably, she was dribbling a pale viscous liquid from the corner of her mouth – perhaps from the carp – and she went to wipe it away, but it wouldn't come off; it just consumed the tissue. The tissues had come from the red envelope. One by one she flushed them down the toilet. In the handsome white porcelain bowl, something was left, something that would not flush away. A small dark pebble-like thing. It was apparently stuck to the porcelain. She went to prize it off, and felt a sharp stab of pain.

'It's a tooth from the carp! It's still alive…!' Qiao realized. She looked at her shell, easy enough to pierce, and felt vaguely distressed.

Yellow Peace Rose

A year after her wedding, Qiao finally got around to clearing a corner of the yard and planting a few rose bushes. A neighbour had given her the clippings and, just as the willows were coming into leaf, Qiao pushed those little twigs into the soil and covered them with glass jars, turning them into a line of gleaming mushrooms. She went out every day to sneak a look, quivering with excitement. One of those days, like a child pulling back a curtain to reveal a technicolour universe of toys, she lifted a jar and was thrilled to see a tiny green bud. Six months later, the jars could no longer contain the burgeoning leafy branches. They were a luminous, waxy green, especially eye-catching against the rest of the grey, unkempt little yard.

There came a point when she no longer dared go near the old maple tree, it was so covered in insects. Popo, her mother-in-law, kept her eyes permanently fixed to the chink between the curtains, and the moment Qiao detected the glint of her hazel irises, her neck went soft. She would shrink away, wishing she could retract her head into her chest and grow a protective shell. The two old luffa gourds from the wedding ceremony had disintegrated and blown around on the wind, their rotting, cotton-like pulp becoming tangled with cobwebs and larvae, slowly seeping into the soil to turn into some other kind of matter. Late at night, they emitted a curious blue glow.

Qiao covered the flowers with the thinnest of plastic membranes.

Moonlight flooded through, bathing the bushes. Every so often, her thoughts would turn to the foul black luffa gourds — usually at bath time, as she watched Popo work a towel back and forth across her damp back, her long, flat breasts sopping wet, drooping all the way to her navel.

None of the older generation ever commented on the roses. The bushes grew and grew. Sometimes her husband, Yuanzhi, would creep out and loosen the soil around their roots, pouring in a little water. At night, when the two of them were alone, they would talk and talk about the flowers, chatting until Qiao could think of nothing else to say. Then they would fall silent. One such night, Yuanzhi leapt up to fetch water for the old folks to wash their feet, urging Qiao to get some sleep. Hovering on the brink of unconsciousness, she became dimly aware of Yuanzhi's grandmother, Taipo, standing at the foot of the bed. Taipo was dressed in black, her grey face devoid of features, and she was staring fixedly at Qiao. Qiao let out a hoarse cry and snapped awake to find herself confronting the clothes rail in the corner of the bedroom, from which hung a collection of black clothes. The room was very dark. The curtains billowed silently, then fell softly back into place.

At some point, the window blew open. Qiao pulled on her slippers and went to close it. It was raining outside, the soft patter of the raindrops muting all other sounds. From the window, Qiao watched blearily as the buds on her rose bushes unfurled into flowers. One, then another, and another, their translucent petals spreading wide open. The rain could have been dripping straight from the stars; the sound was mesmerising. The rose leaves had a dark, glossy sheen, and their stamens were burnished gold, appearing like starry explosions against the night. Qiao stood rooted to the spot, not daring to move. She lost all sense of time. Eventually, a curtain of even thicker darkness swooped down and extinguished the scene. Only then did she softly exhale, as though returned to her senses.

First thing the next morning, Qiao rushed to the yard. Sure enough, the rose bushes were in full bloom. A dazzling array of reds, whites, yellows, pinks, bathed in the hazy gold of the morning sunlight. She gently shook a branch, emptying rainwater from the flowers' faces. Yuanzhi leaned out of the bedroom window, his eyes still gummed with sleep; from deep among the roses, Qiao shot him her most charming smile. Thinking to herself: *At least half this yard belongs to me.*

Taipo was always sneaking food from the kitchen, after which she would fart loudly. The grease on the old cooking pot grew thicker and thicker, and Qiao felt nauseous every time she tried to clean it. One day, when it was full of dense, fat-white soup and the old lady dredged up a pork shoulder, Qiao gagged and ran from the room. Leaning over the bowl of the flush toilet, she vomited again and again, marvelling that there could be anything left to come up. By the end, it was mostly just dirty water. Yuanzhi paced the yard in a panic, unsure what to do. His father, Gonggong, and Taipo were equally at a loss. Only Popo seemed unperturbed, crossing both arms across her washboard-flat chest and twisting her mouth into a smirk. 'Got a bun in her, I'd say.' Gonggong's lips peeled back into a wide grin. He had very good teeth – they put people in mind of the old White Horse Tooth kind of sweetcorn.

Qiao began throwing up constantly, sometimes to the point of passing out. When it came down to it, Yuanzhi was a decent man. He heard that fruit would help and brought home big piles of guanggan oranges, only to have them all turn to mush. Qiao felt hollowed out, like an empty shell of a person, but it was Popo who acted most affronted. She completely stopped smiling. Yuanzhi had no idea why and dared not ask. It wasn't until he was playing mahjong with his grandmother that, in the middle of a perfectly amicable game, she made the gloomy pronouncement, 'With vomit like this, it's bound to be a girl!' No more was spoken about it. Now, when Qiao was in the toilet, the vomit coming in waves, loud one minute, quiet the next, Popo would signal to Yuanzhi with her eyes, and he'd tiptoe over and apologetically close the door.

The flowers in the yard suddenly withered away. One after the other, heads drooping, petals all falling off. Qiao dragged herself outside to look and saw that the bugs from the old maple tree had swarmed over the luffa frame and were now flapping around the rose bushes, blithely sucking the juice from their leaves and flowers. Seeing that Qiao was on the verge of tears, Yuanzhi screwed up his courage and went to talk to his grandmother. When the old woman heard that he wanted to chop down the maple and destroy the luffa trellis, she jabbed a spindly finger at her grandson's nose, too horrified to speak. Her fingernail left a livid crescent on its tip, which took days to fade. Qiao was left watching from the window as the insects gobbled up her precious flowers, astonished by their efficiency. They invaded and devoured, without even realising what they were doing. She knew there was no point in trying to kill them. Even if she killed this lot, more would follow. There was simply nothing to be done.

Eventually, there came a day when the creature inside Qiao seemed to have vomited enough. Qiao's whole body felt light and refreshed. She walked unsteadily into the yard where, among the drifts of dead flowers and decaying leaves, she saw a yellow peace rose, still standing tall. In the slanted rays of sun, it looked like a pure gold crown. She stood without moving a muscle. She did not cry, knowing that there would be four pairs of eyes at the window, fixed on her and this strange yellow rose.

Her baby was born in autumn. It was a boy. Gonggong cracked one of his big, toothy grins. Popo's face was wreathed in smiles. When Qiao arrived home from the maternity hospital with the baby in her arms, his eyes were wide open. Taipo sucked her gums and said, 'He'll be a handful, with eyes wide like that!' And then asked, 'What's his name?'

Qiao smiled and said softly, 'I was thinking of calling him Tinker, because he certainly tinkered about enough with my insides! Caused me no end of troubles.'

Yuanzhi smiled, too. Then, when none of the three older folks responded, hastened to add, 'But Taipo, you should give him a name! That'll help him live a long and prosperous life. Here we are, four generations under one roof! What more could any child wish for...'

Taipo used a long, sharp fingernail to pinch a hawthorn berry off the tree. She popped it into her mouth, closing her eyes as she chewed.

'According to the family tree, this is the Zhong generation,' piped up Gonggong. 'So why not call him Zhong Hua.'

His wife twitched her lips in disapproval.

'Name him when he's older,' she said. 'Leave it till he starts school.'

But Taipo suddenly opened an eye, her wrinkles slipping comically around her face, shifting shape as she pronounced, 'Call him Butt-Ugly, that'll keep him in line.'

Qiao raised her chin defiantly, her eyebrows almost disappearing into her hairline as she looked across at Yuanzhi; Yuanzhi swallowed noisily and hung his head.

And so the child's name remained undecided. Behind closed doors, Qiao still called him Tinker. Every day she sang him eighteen songs, fed him nineteen times, switched twenty dirty nappies for clean ones. Her milk was exceptionally plentiful, gushing like a fountain over the child's face. One suckle and he was already red in the cheeks, practically choking on it. He had a good appetite but slept badly, forever jerking awake at a noise only he could hear. His little black eyes would stare in horror at the clothes rack. Recalling her own, earlier dream, Qiao told Yuanzhi to move the rack out of their room. At noon on one particularly sunny day, she stood by the window with the baby, basking in the warmth. The child's face was so flawlessly pink it could have been powdered on, and he snuggled contentedly into her bosom. Qiao hummed to him under her breath.

All of a sudden, he seemed to sense something and struggled against her; she hurriedly tightened her grip. Following the gaze of his bright, alert little eyes, she looked out of the window. There was nothing there. She moved as though to carry him away, but he burst out crying, forcing her to stay where she was. A little while later, he smiled. His lips pulled out into the sweetest, most beautiful of grins. It really was adorable. Qiao couldn't resist leaning in to kiss it. As she did, she had the feeling her lips were brushing up against the fragrant, tender petals of a rose.

Popo came into the room. Both Popo and Taipo liked to wear black. In the heat of summer, they went about in jackets and trousers of gambiered Canton gauze. Taipo's had started to show its age, the colour leaching to a kind of ochre. She always smelled like camphor. Her daughter, on the other hand, was never less than impeccably turned-out. Slim and graceful. Her long, flat bottom swayed elegantly beneath her slender waist. While Qiao had not yet regained her pre-baby figure, Popo was more alluring than ever, frequently causing Gonggong's jaw to drop open in appreciation, as though preparing himself for a bite.

'Watch out, that sun will burn the child's scalp off!' she exclaimed, swooshing the curtains closed. The baby instantly started to wail as though his heart were breaking.

'He's starving!' she added.

'I've only just fed him,' said Qiao, lightly patting his back, rocking him from side to side.

'Well, then what's he crying for? He obviously wants to suckle.' Beneath her drooping eyelids, Popo's hazel eyes were accusing triangles, boring into Qiao like spikes. Resignedly, Qiao unbuttoned her blouse, but the child carried on wailing and straining towards the window, paying no attention whatsoever to her proffered nipples.

'Your milk must be bad. Quick, try it yourself, see if it's bitter.' Popo waved her long arms for emphasis.

Qiao wished she could bury herself in the pile of decaying leaves and flowers out in the yard. Or else that she could push her mother-in-law into it. She waited a while, and then, almost whispering, said, 'Ma, he wants to look at the rose!'

'Nonsense!' said Popo. 'He's not even one month old, he doesn't know what a rose looks like! Are all your books turning you soft in the head?'

She swept out of the room, picking her way in brisk little steps, stirring up a gust of wind that knocked off a nappy drying over the back of a chair.

From then on, Qiao took advantage of Popo's afternoon naps to fling the curtains wide open. Invariably, her son's bright little eyes would stare determinedly out of the window. Qiao knew what he was looking at: that dazzling, sunshine-yellow peace rose. It wasn't visible from the window but, even so, Qiao knew that he could see it. Children had a way of seeing things that adults couldn't. And anyway, there was that intoxicating rose scent, carrying in on the autumn breeze.

After his one-month birthday celebrations, Tinker bloomed into the handsomest little man that ever there was. His tiny pink face was covered in a fine, powdery down, and a lazy smile was always playing at the edges of his mouth. One flicker in the depths of his black, crystalline eyes, and he seemed in possession of all the world's secrets. His grandparents were over the moon, convinced that they'd landed a prince for a grandson. Only his great-grandmother seemed to disagree, sucking on her gums and maintaining a stony silence. Her eyes turned increasingly gloomy.

By two months, Tinker could roll over; by four, he could sit up. By the time Qiao's maternity leave was over, he was a chubby little boy who could crawl around on the bed. This was the bed Qiao and Yuanzhi had used after their wedding – it was still made up with the same flashy red satin quilt, although they had long since relinquished it to Yuanzhi's parents. Now, however, it had become Tinker's imperial residence. He'd pick up a toy, play with it for a bit, then toss it aside, sure in the knowledge that someone would come rushing to pick it up. He tired quickly of every new plaything and, once he did, reverted to looking out of the window, wailing. Nothing would pacify him.

During one such tantrum, Qiao had the bright idea of quietly turning on her tape recorder, releasing the cheerful plinkety-plonk of some music. Tinker immediately stopped crying and crawled around and around the machine. His eyes glinted; his little hands reached out and pressed the button. As soon as the music sounded, he grinned and clapped. Taipo stuck out her tongue.

When Qiao went back to work, she hired a village girl from Hebei as a nanny. The girl used to strap Tinker to her back while she got on with cooking and doing the laundry. She took charge of the household. Taipo took a shine to her and started thrusting chunks of her savings into the girl's hands, after which the girl was even more conscientious about her work.

One day, another nanny from the neighbourhood brought over a colourful toy dog, which could be taken apart and reassembled, like a puzzle. Once Tinker got his hands on it, his ten little fingers were glued to the dog's bright little body; he wouldn't even pause for milk. He pulled the dog apart, piece by piece, and then put it back together again. He lay on his stomach, plump bottom sticking in the air, its dark birthmark on full display. His shiny black hair resembled the big round head of a chrysanthemum in full bloom.

When Qiao came home from work that day, the first thing she saw was Yuanzhi, Popo and Taipo at the end of the yard, Popo and Taipo dressed in their standard attire of jackets and trousers made from black Canton gauze. They were standing imposingly beneath the old maple tree and Qiao immediately shrank into herself, wishing she could magic a suit of armour and hide herself inside it. But Popo's knife-like gaze was already slashing ruthlessly up and down her body. She tried to slip past them into the house, only to be blocked by Taipo's wide black sleeve. The old lady grabbed her by the wrist, leaving a pale pink welt on the skin. It was unbearably itchy.

'What's...is something wrong?'

'No, no, nothing's...' Yuanzhi stammered, glancing nervously at the three older folks. 'You...*cough*...Tinker, no, I mean, the baby...how did you get pregnant with the baby?'

Qiao stared in disbelief. She couldn't take in what Yuanzhi was saying. She could hear his grandmother, inside the house now, farting, and following it up with a long, heavy sigh.

'Don't you worry, don't you go making yourself ill,' Popo called in to the old lady.

Tinker was fast asleep, his little rosebud mouth half-open, his tiny nose gently flaring as he breathed. His long black eyelashes spilled onto his powder-perfect cheeks. Beside him lay the multi-coloured puzzle dog, with its big droopy ears.

'He put it together all by himself,' said the nanny, whispering into Qiao's ear. 'His granny is worried he's too sharp, that he'll be trouble to raise!'

Somehow, the yellow peace rose flourished. It was odd, because the insects got to all the other rose bushes, gnawing them right down to their roots. But the peace rose clung on, getting taller by the day, sprouting new branches, every new bud as exquisitely beautiful as the last. One sunny day, the nanny brought the little boy out into the yard to play. He fastened his eyes to the peace rose, refusing to budge. Observing the scene from the window, his grandmother came out and picked one of the flowers for him. He rolled it around in his little hands, shaking out the dew. The sunlight was soft and honeyed, draping itself around the flower like a fine silk cloth, drying off the petals. The stamens curled like the antennae of a butterfly. Tinker stared and stared and then suddenly whispered, 'Ma!'

It was a whisper, but still loud enough for Popo and the nanny to hear. Popo hurriedly picked him up. 'Good boy,' she crooned, 'that's a flower, not your Ma!'

But Tinker said it again, this time louder and clearer. 'Ma!'

Popo's eyelids drooped with annoyance and she called to the nanny. 'You need to teach him names! Teach him to say Taipo! And then

Popo and Gonggong.'

On hearing that her son could say 'Ma', Qiao smothered him in kisses. But Tinker kept on using it for the flowers. The nanny noticed that he'd say it once first thing in the morning, and that would be for Qiao. In the afternoons, however, he'd say it over and over again, as though his very life depended on it – and that meant he wanted to go out to the flowers. At first, Popo corrected him, but eventually she gave up, changing her opinion of her formerly beloved grandson, declaring him a little bastard. At night, she confided her concerns to her husband, hissing into his ear from between her teeth, even managing to squeeze out a few pearly tears.

Since the arrival of her great-grandson, Taipo had been stealing less food, and therefore farting a little less often. She even seemed a little livelier. The nanny had a magic touch – noticing how the old lady spent all day keeping watch, she gently, patiently taught Tinker to say, 'Taipo! Popo! Gonggong!' It cheered Taipo, and meant she'd scoop a bowl of her fatty pork shoulder soup for the nanny, filling it right to the brim. The nanny would slurp the whole thing down and still have room for more. As time wore on, she started helping herself from the pot; after a while, she helped herself to whatever she felt like. Taipo did not seem to notice. Her belly full of her ill-gotten gains, the nanny's cheeks grew rosy, and her energy surged. She giggled uncontrollably whenever she saw Yuanzhi.

The little boy could call all the old folk by name, but no longer said 'Ma'. Popo made a special trip into town, investing in fabric that cost two whole clothing coupons per foot, which she instructed Qiao to make up into an outfit for the nanny. The fabric was clearly designed to be a curtain. Two ferns ran up and down either side, and the middle was filled with very bright flowers. It was thin but heavily starched, so that it felt stiff to touch. When the nanny saw it, her eyes narrowed to crescents as she screwed her mouth into a sweet smile. Qiao took her measurements and carefully cut the fabric, edged it, pinned it, then had to study it and pin again, trying to make the fabric go further.

Once it was sewn together and the nanny tried it on, it pulled at the seams, straining over her generous bosom, its skirt over her backside as taut as a dumpling wrapper.

The little boy cocked his head and stared and stared, his black eyes spinning. After a while, he lifted one side of his mouth into a lopsided smile, as though he knew everything there was to know, causing everyone to smile along with him.

'There's something odd about this child!' said Popo, waving her loose sleeves of black Canton gauze. 'We should find him a wife as soon as possible, so his great-granny can meet the fifth generation!'

Gonggong's laugh sounded like a horse neighing. And, at that, they all started laughing so hard that they could barely breathe, making poor Qiao – who was inside, pressing the dress – almost jump out of her skin.

On Tinker's first birthday, Qiao rushed to the shopping mall after work to buy him some toys. She arrived home full of excitement, only to open the door and find the house filled with people – and her son hemmed in by the crowd, a livid red crest sprouting from his head, floppy and discoloured from the sun. A random assortment of garish, shiny tails had been pinned to his bottom and hung there, swinging between his legs. Qiao was so horrified that she wanted to scream. She hurriedly brought a finger to her mouth and bit down hard. Then the human fence started to disperse, and she saw that Tinker was actually wearing a vermillion satin cap, and that what she'd thought was a tail was actually a cotton baby wrapper, intricately embroidered with dragons. The chubby infant was too dressed up to move; he was sprawled on a rattan chair, looking every bit the little emperor. He appeared unmoved by Qiao's entrance, glancing at her only briefly. She froze where she was, hugging her bag of toys. No one seemed aware that she was the mother of this child, and no one came over to introduce her.

The crowd feasted their eyes and gorged their bellies until well into the night. Qiao bent her slender neck and set about tidying a dislodged mat, trying not to catch anyone's eye. A lady of about fifty poked at her teeth with a toothpick, her eyes bright, her lips twisting as she spoke, 'The child is positively thriving! Whose milk has he been drinking, to grow so big?'

Popo glanced at Gonggong. There was a brief pause, and then she replied, beaming, 'Oh, he drinks cow's milk!'

The lady pursed her lips in surprise. 'My goodness, I've never seen a child grow like that on cow's milk!'

Qiao looked wide-eyed at her in-laws, and then at Yuanzhi, who simply hung his head. She was so preoccupied with staring at him that she let the fish bone she was holding fall to the floor.

Qiao contracted a strange illness. Her neck felt perpetually weak, compelling her to keep it pulled into her chest. Even around her son, she didn't dare extend it. A kind of mocking expression crept onto the child's delicate pink face when she was around him, and she had the feeling that her skin was slowly hardening, like armour. That nothing could hurt her anymore. She became extremely lazy. Her hair was messy and her face went unwashed, without a speck of makeup. She left her beloved yellow peace rose untended, and the yard reverted to its former state – the bug-ridden luffa trellis spread until it had swallowed the rosebush, and Qiao couldn't muster the energy to care. She ate much more than she used to and gained weight. While she was in the toilet, she would look at herself in the mirror. The silver behind the glass was almost gone, making her reflection blurry, but still she could see that she was so fat the wrinkles on her face had stretched out, pulling her skin so taut she looked made of wax. It was a horrifying sight, and she tried to avert her eyes. Then came the thought that it wasn't really her in the mirror. That it wasn't a real person, it was a fake. Someone she didn't know and never had. She pulled the mirror closer, to look more carefully, but her breath fogged over the face, leaving only a shadow. A featureless grey blob.

Her son often sat drawing at the long table outside the house. At two and a half, he started nursery school. He could draw many things. The young nanny had long since left, having gone home to get married. Taipo had taken out all her old bridal clothes to give to her, considering it an act of charity towards a poor village girl. Only, the next day, the clothes were exactly where she'd left them, and her savings were short a few dozen kuai. Once she'd caught her breath, she went to whinge and wail to Popo, but in the end that was as far as it went.

Qiao would sit at the other end of the bench to her son, knitting. One such evening, she looked at him very seriously and said, 'Tinker, will you draw Mummy a flower?'

'What kind of flower?' he asked.

'That yellow peace rose we used to have in the yard. You used to love that rose, when you were little.'

'What yellow peace rose?' asked the boy, coldly.

And Qiao realised those black, crystalline eyes had transformed into two lumps of ice. She went back to her room and pulled apart the sweater she'd been working on. Pulled it apart row by row, the loosened wool as twisted as curls of shaved iron. It piled up into a steely purple cobweb, with her buried at its centre. She thought of the two luffa gourds in the yard after her wedding, blackened and rotting, and how the whole yard had been full of insects and their eggs. It filled her with a malicious delight. She smiled.

The boy's drawing got better and better. One day, he drew a giant horse, a tiny mouse and two black crows, one big and fat, one small and skinny, and ran back and forth through the house, showing it to everyone. His grandparents and Yuanzhi clustered around, overjoyed by his handiwork. By this stage Taipo was nearing ninety, but her hooded eyes remained intimidatingly bright. The boy explained to the adults what he had drawn, saying that the two ravens were Taipo and

Popo, the horse was Gonggong, and his daddy was the tiny mouse. There was no mummy.

The adults stared at the picture for a while, until it finally dawned on Popo what it meant. She beamed with delight, gripping Taipo's veiny arm, their fluttery black sleeves tangling together.

'Ma, the child has drawn us as crows, and his grandpa as a dashing stallion!' She was almost shouting, she was so happy. 'There's no doubt you'll live a long life now, with animals as lucky as these!'

Taipo squinted, then nodded and smiled. 'He is a sweet child, after all. Look, Yuanzhi is a tiger!'

'That's right!' Popo grinned, revealing a mouth of fang-like teeth. Qiao slipped away to watch quietly from the sidelines.

'Ha! The child has drawn you as phoenixes! But you haven't noticed yet, you can't see it!'

Gonggong had a strange laugh, like a horse neighing. He laughed so long and hard that his pink gums showed, and Qiao noticed for the first time that he wore false teeth. They shook in his mouth, as though about to leap out. And, at that, Qiao started to join in – she laughed until tears formed in her eyes. Popo was grinning and holding Tinker, rocking him and smothering him in kisses. His tender little face was so drenched in her loving saliva that it appeared deformed. He stared in alarm at the universe of hysterical adults all around him, until eventually he burst out crying.

He stopped drawing after that. Whatever the other children were doing, he did too. This was a weight off Taipo's mind.

'He should be like other children! He was getting too clever for his own good. Clever children are more trouble than they're worth!'

A few years later, the boy started primary school, where he was exceptionally well-behaved. He was also popular among his peers, and respectful to his elders. He always did what he was told. People were forever praising him for being such a good little boy. When the neighbours were telling off their children, they used him as an example. 'You should be more like Tinker!' they would say, and Tinker's grandparents would glow pink with pride.

Taipo was still going strong, concerned with her great grandson's every move. Her greasy old casserole pot went on stewing, and Qiao would scrub and scrub, but could never rid it of its lingering burnt smell. The old lady complained about it often, even while ladling out scoops of greasy, acrid-smelling broth – which, inevitably, would be followed by one of her noxious farts. Even from two rooms away, Qiao could still smell them. One day, she had the sudden thought that those poisonous odours might have killed the yellow peace rose and, that night, she crept out to examine the flowerbed. The blue light of her torch illuminated a nest of writhing white maggots. They clustered, they collided, they squeezed into and over one another, every so often converging into one big mass, wriggling into the earth. Qiao smartly patted down the earth, and never thought of the rose again.

Her son grew ever more charming and delightful. He could not have been closer to his three grandparents and got along well with his father. But he treated his mother like a stranger. On the rare occasions that he did address her, his 'Ma' was hesitant, as though masking some underlying embarrassment. And his once-bright eyes had lost some of their lustre. They remained beautiful, but there was a chilling frostiness to them. One night, Qiao couldn't sleep, and heard movement in the bedroom on the other side of the wall.

'I always said he wasn't like other people's grandsons!' came Popo's strident voice.

'Whaddya mean not like…grandsons?' Gonggong slurred his words, sounding on the verge of sleep.

'I mean he's different!'

'Mmm.'

'There's something about him. Who knows what rank official he'll end up as in future!'

Qiao heard her chuckle under her breath.

What Qiao couldn't have known was that the boy had his secrets. He had dreamed of an enormous rose. No, an enormous rose bush, and at its very top was a giant yellow flower. The sun covered the flower like molten glass, turning the petals translucent, making them look as though they were melting into a hazy golden blur. There was a light breeze, gently stirring the petals, causing an odd tinkling sound. He moved closer and saw that each leaf had transformed into a transparent little bell, and the dewdrops that had been on the leaves were now tiny stars, circling around the bush. Drawing closer still, he could hear that the rose was sighing. When he touched the leaves, they were warm. The rose's golden stamen stretched majestically upwards, surrounded by dancing pistils. The yellow rose was so beautiful, and the boy stood on his tiptoes, trying desperately to reach it, to no avail. He brought over a ladder and climbed it rung by rung, but when he made it to the middle, it collapsed from under him. He awoke with a start, cried, 'Ah!' and then, just once, 'Ma!'

Poor Qiao, she was fast asleep by then. She didn't hear him.

The Art Gallery

1

The sky was new. So new it looked fake, as though slick and glistening from the wash. The blue had faded, but that was only to be expected – and on a morning with sunshine as splendid as this, even a clean, grey sky was cause for delight.

She wore a long black gown. Her gloves and boots were scarlet. As she walked into the gallery, she glanced down at the boots, causing the lady at the ticket counter to glance down too. Mistrust and disdain flared in the ticket lady's eyes.

She knew she was beautiful. Or, to be precise, that she used to be beautiful. She wore this dazzling shade of red as a challenge to her age. She had never been one to shy away from a challenge, an attitude that kept her perpetually on edge – for decades, she had existed in a state of relentless anxiety, and as a result had avoided getting fat. This was not necessarily a good thing. There comes an age when, if a woman does not get fat, she gets skinny. Not slim in the supple, vital way of younger women, but withered and dried-out. As she was now. Her skin was still fair, but fair like a sheet of old parchment, ready to crinkle at the first breath of wind. Viewed from afar, surrounded by the earthy tones of the sculptures, she was captivating: black and scarlet unsullied by a single speck of dust, her skin a brilliant white. Only she knew that the white was one kind of a mask, and the black and scarlet another. Come evening, she would face the mirror and peel back the layers, until finally she saw herself as she truly was.

The gallery felt so outdated! It had been built the year she was born. Back then, the glazed yellow roof tiles were offset by a glazed blue sky. In the plum blossom trees outside, she had once caught an enormous butterfly, whose wings were almost alarmingly bright: pristine red and black, along with a powdery, snowy white. She had carefully pressed it into her diary. Its colours bled through the pages, and gradually it withered away, shrinking into itself until it was a colourful, dried-out stain, as though gathering close a whole lifetime of flying. Then it started to fade and became so brittle that one touch seemed enough to shatter it. At this point, she shoved the diary to the back of a desk drawer, defeated by the exquisite cruelty of such an ending, considering that the end of the tale of the butterfly.

The diary languished in the dark recesses of the drawer. Time went by, and a Dell computer took up residence on her desk. She often woke in the middle of the night and went to hunch over it, clicking through the internet, entertaining herself with tales of celebrity sex scandals and far-off wars. On such nights, she did not turn on the lights. The night was far from simply black, she discovered; there was a jade-like quality to the darkness, like a submerged aquatic plant, with that same, moist beauty. And when that moisture set in, she found herself stopping, taking a deep breath. As she was now – in the gallery, facing all those strange and wonderful sculptures.

2

The gallery walls were tall and imposing, and entirely unadorned. The windows were set very high up. From where she was standing, she could see three of the walls. They were a cold grey colour. Beside a window, beneath an African totem, was a giant advertisement, in English and Chinese. A mystifying series of numbers was written across it, ordered from largest to smallest, although she couldn't see exactly how low they went. Quite a few were blocked by sculptures of women from the other side of the world, where the sun was like an alchemist. Scalding hot, scorching their skin, roasting their bodies, until they could stand here like this, naked or half-naked, their sensual lips closed or slightly parted, shamelessly exposing their beautiful bronzed breasts. It occurred to her that, in that sun-baked place, there was no Li Bai waxing lyrical about the moon, no tragic legend of ill-fated butterfly lovers. On long, melancholy nights, there was no running to the theatre to take solace in bleak love dramas.

Love. She felt assaulted by her own, unintentional choice of words.

Love had ended for her in the late nineties. After another meaningless entanglement, she said to herself, *Enough*. No more of that searing agony and hidden, aching yearning. Every inch of her dried out, to the point that there were no tears left in her eyes. That was when she realised love was really a kind of liquid; a magical liquid. When it disappeared, old age set in.

Every day, she lamented the lack of moisture in her skin, how it was somehow vanishing, from one minute to the next. There was no way to stop it. She finally understood the butterfly; how even the most vivid beauty is temporary and will fade away.

One evening, in the jade-tinged darkness, she gently pulled open the desk drawer. Her heart pounded as she opened the dust-covered diary, as if sensing that something was about to happen. With trepidation sitting heavily on her shoulders, she turned the brittle, yellowing pages. The butterfly was gone; there remained only a few blackened chrysalises, which seemed to be staring at her ominously. Somehow, the butterfly had managed to lay eggs, which had hatched into caterpillars, which had pupated.

She covered her mouth to muffle a scream. Then she snapped shut the diary and hurled it back into the farthest reaches of the drawer. She locked the drawer with a key. *I should throw away the drawer and burn it*, she thought to herself. But she wanted someone else to do it, not her.

3

Some time later, she noticed the gallery tiling. This was no ordinary tiling: the tiles were polygons but irregular in shape, like kites or the heads of darts, hundreds of them, and pieced together into a wonderful geometric design. It was arranged on the diagonal, making the confined space appear to stretch out to infinity. She started counting the tiles as she walked across them, trying to work out which one she was standing on. But she quickly discovered that, no matter how far she walked, she couldn't distinguish where one tile ended and another began.

Her thoughts turned to that nineties love affair, the one that had put an end to all others. One night (she had not yet discovered the jade quality of darkness), the object of her affections, a physicist, had tested her.

'If you lived in a circular town of any given size, how far would you need to walk before finding yourself in an identical one?'

She thought for a bit, and then said, 'I don't know.'

The physicist seemed to be expecting this. He looked out of the window, puffing slowly on a cigarette.

She waited and waited for him to reply, until eventually she could bear it no longer – 'Come on!' she said. 'What's the answer?'

He slowly stubbed out his cigarette. 'To be honest, I don't know either.'

By that point, their affair was already nearing its end.

4

For as long as she could remember, she had been terrified of intimate relationships with the opposite sex. As a young woman, she had been afraid of getting hurt, but now her biggest worry was that she had lost the ability to love anyone at all. Whenever she met a man, she was like an x-ray device, scanning him for deficiencies. And what followed was pure acting on her part: she had to pretend that everything was fine, then find a way to vanish. It was the exact opposite of her younger days, because she no longer feared being hurt; she feared hurting other people. But when it came down to it, both states were exhausting.

She tried with the same sex but found it even more horrifying. There are so many hidden ravines between women; one misunderstanding, and you fall right in. Sometimes, a single sentence – even just a glance – is enough to create a bomb, ready to explode.

The outside world is so full of wonders and yet so helpless, so dangerous. But after she retreated from it into her own, interior world, she realised things there were much worse. In a garden flat in the north of the city, she discovered there existed so many versions of herself, each one barking out a constant stream of orders, and she didn't know which one to listen to. Her anticipated freedom did not materialise. Everything she tried to do to 'move on' was executed poorly and inappropriately, as though she were being intensely observed and it was making her clumsy.

She instantly regretted every single thing she did, because every single time she made mistakes. For example, she always intended to bring the garbage out with her when she went to exercise in the morning, then go to buy fresh milk and come home for breakfast. Every morning, these were the only things she had to think about. It was a perfectly good plan. But, so often, she would come home and see the garbage still lying there, or else realise that she'd forgotten to buy milk. In fact, in all the years that this had been her plan for the morning, she had never once managed to pull it off without a hitch. Her good intentions were constantly betrayed by the clumsiness of her actions – and this was just one of the more minor examples.

She thought of her ex-husband, a pasty, overweight man who was nevertheless very practical. That's to say, lacking in both mind and spirit but quick with his hands, which was possibly the reason their marriage had lasted for fifteen years. Eventually, she realised that his deftness extended mainly to handling chickens and turtles, or to reconnecting wires after a blown fuse. Once, overwhelmed with work, she had asked him to help her with an insect specimen, only for the poor insect to end up minus a wing. Her husband hadn't apologised. In fact, he hadn't even mentioned it, just left her to find out for herself. And when she had, a chill rose from the soles of her feet, travelling all the way to her throat, where it choked her, leaving her unable to speak. After a while, when it relaxed its grip a little, she tried again. 'What happened to the wing?'

At which the pasty, tubby fellow leapt up, suddenly quick as a flash. 'How dare you! I helped you, didn't I? I helped you and now all you can do is complain!'

'The wing has broken off,' she said. 'Now the whole specimen is ruined.'

He grabbed the specimen and marched towards the bathroom. 'All this fuss over one stupid bug? Fine, fine...let's just throw the whole fucking thing away then, shall we? You said it was ruined, didn't you?'

She did not move. She was not a girl any longer and had no talent for acting. All she could do was keep sitting there, waiting for the clatter that meant the insect and its glass petri dish had flown to the bottom of the building.

Of course, this alone was no grounds for divorce. The divorce process ended up being extremely complicated and drawn-out. She remembered an autobiography she had read about fifteen years before, of a well-known woman writer (back then, the whole country seemed to be reading fiction; one good novel was enough to make a person famous). This writer talked about going for a stroll in Beijing's Fragrant Hills Park with her husband. Out of nowhere, he started talking about the price of yellowfin croakers, and because of that she decided to divorce him. Thinking about it now, there must have been more to it than that. If she really did divorce over yellowfin croakers – well, then that writer should count herself lucky.

5

Where the hall rounded a corner, the darts and kites turned into birds and fish. The ones flying up the wall were birds, and the ones plunging into the floor were fish. The corner's little secret.

She could not work out how exactly they changed. There was no discernible process of transformation. She felt the same way while listening to Bach's canons, unable to understand how they could soar like that and still return to the same point. A line of kites and darts ran through the middle of the birds and fishes, acting a little like sign posts – like arrowheads, in fact, pointing either up or down. Up, and they became birds; down and they became fish.

Fish or birds, either way they were lucky. The scary thing was, poised like that at the turn in the hall, they became signposts for other people's routes.

6

At the turn in the hall, visitors swarmed around an African girl with a jar of water on her head. Her posture was astonishing; from a distance, she looked like a beautiful, distorted sika deer. It was only at midday, when the crowd dispersed for lunch, that the statue was fully revealed. She strolled over to it, staring at this girl. Examining her.

When she finally turned to a different exhibit, she had the feeling that someone was following her. Softly. Like a shadow.

A pair of mud-splattered feet shifted to one side of her and, softly, playfully, as though by accident, she stepped on one of them. The foot dropped a few grains of brown dust, then disappeared. Perhaps she was imagining it, but when she spun around to look, she thought she glimpsed a lanky brown figure vanishing through the next glass door. She chased after it. As she ran, she saw from the corner of her eyes that the girl with the jar on her head had disappeared.

She followed a long thin puddle of water. At the turn in the hall, the puddle changed shape, soaking into the kites and darts and seeping towards the fish and the birds.

Would the girl have gone the way of the fish or way of the birds? Either way, the outcome would be the same. When she reached the third exhibition room, she saw the figure again, her long legs striding unhurriedly ahead.

7

'Come back! Come back!' In her head, she was shouting. The girl had been so easily tricked. Or, to be precise, led astray, by those deceptive signposts. They had led her into another exhibition room, into the realm of Escher. The girl was not allowed in there; it was an infringement of the great master's work.

The fish and the birds seemed to pass through one another, switching places as they went, turning into the opposite of what they were when they started, and they could do so because they were the very same thing. Ferocious fish mouths bit the heads of the birds, but in the end the blood came from their very own tails.

Isomorphic!

Yes, isomorphic! That was the secret.

One of those jade-tinged nights, the physicist had said, 'Isomorphic.'

When she thought about it now, the word had a sheen to it. *Isomorphic.*

Escher was making use of the intrinsic similarity of the images to turn the fish into birds. They passed through the kites and darts and, in the process, one image was projected into the other and the identical information they each carried with them made them isomorphs.

'So, is this also the secret of humankind?'

'Yes. And now you understand this, surely you feel some hope for humanity?'

'No,' she said. 'Quite the opposite. I feel even more despairing.'

What she meant was: she'd suddenly realised that her fat pasty husband and the physicist right in front of her were carriers of identical human make-ups. They too were isomorphs.

8

Another World is gorgeous.

Behind its black and white detailing, there's a splash of green, in the form of the jade-tinged night. It's another isomorphic design. The two identical images are like a photograph and its negative, or a yin-yang symbol. In them both, the subject is an elongated human head and a dove: one is the negative of the other; one is the yin, one is the yang. Escher's head looks like a Peking opera mannequin without its wig – elegant, good-natured. The setting is a palace with pillars and a beautiful vaulted roof. It's drawn according to a strictly geometrical design, the perspective so accurate that it could be used as a blueprint. But from such a precisely-detailed blueprint emerges a scene that's rationally impossible: the floor is the cratered surface of the moon and standing on it is a dove with a long human face, but on the arch above stands another version of the dove. A ram's horn hangs from the arch. Beyond the arch, the moon has vanished into the night, replaced by a dim jade-green, staining the black sky. That's from another moon beyond the moon. Serene, mysterious, bizarre. Outside of human comprehension.

Nocturnal Rome
A man in a pointed hat rides a horse through the inky black streets of Rome. Perhaps he is a prince, fallen on hard times. His horse has its hooves raised and its eyes trained straight ahead. His silhouette is slowly melting away – looking into the distance, it's as though a translucent chunk of jade is floating up from the depths of the darkness.

Dream
Another vaulted ceiling, perhaps from the very same palace as *Another World*. A figure sleeps beside a carved pillar, while an enormous praying mantis raises two blade-like legs, as though about to slice into the man's chest. The man is entirely oblivious. He is also wearing a long pointed hat. It's reminiscent of one worn by that famous poet,

the one who went mad and killed himself a few years ago. Apparently, he was very short and wore big hats to appear taller, but without it, he used to hide under tables. From this you can see how important height is for men. If they aren't tall, they have to hide.

9

The girl disappeared on the stairs to the second floor.

The long puddle of water suddenly dried up.

The girl disappeared at the exact moment that the birds and the fish merged together and transformed. Yes, disappeared. The famous poet's wife, once a girl herself, also disappeared. Just like that.

Back when the poet's wife was still a pretty young woman, she was unlucky enough to meet the poet (although, naturally, at the time she considered herself lucky). The poet followed her to her hometown, where he declared his love for her with a passion seldom seen in Chinese men. For a moment, she probably felt the luckiest woman alive, but what good did that do her? It just made the ending all the more bitter.

In the name of love, she gradually withdrew from the world: her misanthropic husband wanted to forsake society and live alone, so they left for a tiny uninhabited island; her eccentric husband did not want to lay eyes on his own son, so she sent the poor little mite to be raised by a friend; her romantic husband wanted to be with two women at the same time, so she brought a young women called Ying'er into their home, and watched the two of them make love with a big fake smile on her face.

She didn't want to hurt him and did everything she could to cater to his demands, but quietly, ever so quietly – careful not to alarm him – she withdrew. While he bathed narcissistically in the beauty of his own writing, describing in exquisite detail the tenderness of Ying'er's genitals, she made her escape. But he wouldn't let her get away with it. His sharp axe was covered in her blood. Her blood spurted out of her body in a powerful stream. He had severed her carotid artery but, even as she drew her last breath, she remained fully conscious. What horror! Her blood sprayed onto his tall hat. His tall white hat and robe were completely soaked. His poetic, 'searching for the light on a dark night' eyes had turned crazed and brutal. She could no longer speak. Her pretty cheeks slowly caved in and her sparkling eyes slowly dulled, but she was not afraid; he was the frightened one. He feared her eyes, and the life he had destroyed. He sprinted to a large tree and hung himself with a rope, but even in his final moments, he demonstrated his stupidity, calling out to his wife for help, as was his wont. This time he cried, 'Help me! Help me hang myself!' He would not let her go; not even death would set her free.

Poets are forever concocting murders during twilight drinking sessions.

There was another poet – a friend of the aforementioned poet; let's call him Poet B, and the first one Poet A. These poets, they just float down from the sky, like little amber islets, and the women, they come flocking.

And so, of course, there was another beautiful woman.

This woman was extremely graceful, with a somewhat melancholy expression. She worked in a factory on the outskirts of town, but she didn't look like a factory girl. Sitting quietly, she called to mind a Russian girl from an oil painting by Vrubel, with that same, sad beauty. Outfits in that era were very plain. She wore the same short jacket all year round, covered with an old, red shawl. She seemed very proud of her poet husband, speaking of him in adoring tones, saying things like: 'He never writes anything lightly. He would rather write nothing at all than write a bad poem.' She spoke very softly, as though slightly short of breath.

But, one year on, she was no longer gracing the earth with her presence. And her death was just as miserable as the last.

One day, the woman's former lover turned up from out of town. Poet B acted welcoming towards him, bustling about making dumplings, debating with the woman about whether to use radish for the filling or fennel. In the end, they agreed to make half and half. Once they had reached a decision, the process began in earnest: rinsing the vegetables, chopping the vegetables, squeezing out the water, mixing the ingredients, and then heating the chili oil and frying the dumplings until they were cooked right through, puffing their mouth-watering steam. At that stage, Poet B couldn't resist a little drink; the other man joined him. The woman decided to have a sip herself – and so it started. They drank a lot. Three jugs of Shaoxing rice wine, six bottles of beer, and then Poet B brought out the home brew he had been fermenting for several years. They drank such a mix that in the end they barely touched the dumplings. The three of them swayed unsteadily, but the woman hadn't forgotten to make up a bed. A camp bed. The camp bed was in the guest room, where naturally the guest was supposed to sleep. So far, nothing about this tale is particularly out of the ordinary. The trouble starts now. Poet B awoke in the night, his tongue thick with soured wine, and when he opened his bleary eyes, his wife was nowhere to be seen. According to him, that's when he knew something was going on. He pushed open the screen door and saw the man hunched over his wife, pounding himself into her. She was moaning softly, her face deathly pale. At the sight of Poet B, the man fell to his knees. The woman's face turned even paler and she looked contemptuously at the kneeling man, her face pained yet resolute. Perhaps emboldened by man's bent knees, the poet unleashed a roar that reverberated through their sixteen-storey tower block. Within seconds, he had ripped the bedding from beneath the sorry pair and thrown it from the window.

'I will not tolerate this filth in my house!' he howled.

The woman did not make a sound, but the expression on her deathly-pale face remained just the same: pained, resolute.

This makes for a chilling story, does it not? For a once-adoring wife to reach such a point!

After this incident, Poet B claimed his wife was mentally ill. He asked the man who had arranged their marriage to start preparing their divorce. His wife did not object or cause any trouble. She simply signed the papers and announced, 'I haven't been to work for such a long time. Tomorrow I'll go back.'

That same evening, Poet B stayed up chatting to the matchmaker, their voices filtering through to the living room. For quite some time now, this was where his wife had been sleeping. Later, when the two men had finally fallen quiet, they heard a strange noise. Exchanging frightened glances, they went reluctantly into the living room, each urging the other to go first. The woman was on the sofa, bundled up in a military overcoat. She was leaning to one side as though sleeping, her face pale and her cheeks a little sunken; they assumed the noise had come from her, crying out in a dream. Poet B quickly checked her wrists, but they were unharmed (she had a history of suicide attempts). The men looked at one another, and Poet B said, 'Perhaps she's sick. Should we call a doctor?' The matchmaker volunteered to fetch one, but just as he reached the bottom of the staircase, he heard Poet B's anguished cry. A primal, inhuman howl.

The matchmaker raced back upstairs, opened the door, and stood rooted to the spot. He had never seen so much blood in all his life! Blood spurted like a fountain, right up to the ceiling. Who knew one body could produce so much blood! Thick, sticky blood, spraying all over the walls. No amount of scrubbing would ever get it off. Poet B was baying like a wolf. 'She cut right through the artery on both sides! What was she thinking? What on earth was she thinking?'

She had been clever about it: she had wrapped herself in that thick padded coat, and it was only when the coat was opened that the blood gushed out. This was her way of taking revenge on the poet. When a woman rebels, you know about it, whether she takes a hard line or a soft one.

Of course, we only have Poet B's word for it. Perhaps another observer would tell a different story. But, in this case, the lips of the lead character will be eternally sealed.

10

At the entrance to the basement, the beautiful, deer-like girl spun around to face her, and then started walking over.

She was wearing a mask of bronze and pure gold, decorated with animal skins, feathers, bullet casings and gemstones. It was both gorgeous and fearsome. In the place where her eyebrows would have been, there were two strips of gold leaf inlaid like crowns. Two roosters were engraved on the cheeks, with sapphires inset for eyes. The mask's nose was daubed with white paint – this stuck her as strange, because in African folklore, white was associated with death.

Was that what this young woman stood for? Was she Death?

It was an alarming thought. But, at the same time, the mask was mesmerisingly beautiful, emanating an intoxicating, walnut wood aroma. Death and beauty had merged, and the result was an overpowering, irresistible attraction.

She desperately wanted a closer look.

In the formative stage of Nile Valley civilisation, singing griots left local villages and created the first historical accounts from ebony, copperplates, botanical fibres, gold and diamonds. Hunting era humans were shown adorned with spears, axes and knives, amid antelopes, rhinoceroses, wild sheep and ostriches. Then came the chariot era, its chariots depicted in fine detail, a horse yoked to every one, daggers hanging from the forearm of every driver. During equestrian times, those horse drivers became riders, sporting feathered helmets. Rock carvings from this period show the emergence of Berber script, which went on to develop a more sophisticated orthography over the course of the camel era. Strangely enough, African art from these early periods rarely features human heads with distinguishable facial features. It was only later that masks began to make an appearance. How did that come about? Were they conceived to scare off wild animals, for decoration, or perhaps as symbols of authority? That queen mask really was almost perfect; it was no wonder the English had stolen it for the British Museum. Unable to retrieve it, the Africans had been compelled to make another one. That was the one on display in the gallery. But it didn't look anything like as beautiful as the mask this girl was wearing now. The reproduction was a man-made creation, but this aromatic gold sensation could only have been made by gods.

Whose idea had it been, to run the Escher exhibition alongside the African one? Even if it was a coincidence, it was odd – isomorphism and masks, the commonplace and the extraordinary, repetition and exception. This young woman, anatomically virtually identical to her, transformed completely by a mask into a person unlike any other. A majestic crane among a flock of chickens.

The young woman was still walking towards her. Drawing nearer and nearer.

She bided her time, staring at the mask as though hypnotised.

When it came close enough to touch, she reached out and lifted it up. Bronze, gold, inlaid with precious stones and, for one, chilling moment, blindingly bright.

11

The next morning, when the gallery cleaner was sweeping the underground exhibition space, she discovered the statue of the African girl, missing for several days. It was lying prone by the entrance; from a distance, it looked like a corpse.

The cleaner reacted as characters in foreign films do when encountering these kinds of scenes. First, she screamed at the top of her lungs. Then she prodded gently at the statue with the tip of her broom. Just a little knock, but enough to loosen some ochre dust. It had looked so sturdy, but here it was, disintegrating just like that. 'My god!' exclaimed the cleaner, realising she had tampered with a crime scene. And just then she heard the footsteps, approaching from all directions.

12

The woman who lived in a garden flat in the northern part of the city was very late paying her management fee. Mr Zhang, the building manager, was at the end of his patience and went to call on her in person. She did not respond to her doorbell. The neighbours said they hadn't seen her in days. Mr Zhang started to feel a little alarmed, recalling old news stories about attacks on single women in garden flats, and hurriedly called over Mr Li. The two men knocked and knocked but still there came no response. In the end, they decided to let themselves in with the spare key.

There was no one inside. A long black gown and a pair of bright scarlet gloves hung over the back of an empty chair, next to which was a pair of scarlet boots. Mr Zhang and Mr Li both remembered that outfit well.

They decided to alert the police. And so, just as night began drawing in, a siren sounded outside the building.

The search continued late into the night, without uncovering a single clue. Ultimately, it was boredom that drove Mr Li to open the drawer. The search party stood around transfixed as a huge flock of butterflies suddenly flew up from the desk. They were almost painfully magnificent, shimmering in the darkness, flapping their wings, beating them against those dazed wooden faces, scattering dust into their gaping mouths.

That particular night was not pure black; there was a jade-like quality to the darkness, like a submerged aquatic plant, with that same, moist beauty.

THE STORY OF A SECRET KEY

One day in April when spring was in the air, I came across a book on a street vendor's stall. It was a tatty old book. The cover was black, with ancient-looking brown-ochre writing, the title half-erased, the only words still legible being rather unusual: 'Secret Key'. This tatty old book stood out like a sore thumb amid the gaudy covers of its companions on the shelf. But that was the very reason why I picked it up. I leafed through it, finally saying to the increasingly impatient salesgirl: 'I'd like to buy this, could you get me out two copies, so I can choose one?' She stuck her upper lip out till it almost reached her nose: 'Sorry, that's the only one left.' 'But it's in such bad condition, it won't be long before you can't sell it at all.' But she shook her head firmly. 'Will you let me have a discount, then?' I pursued. But the girl must have seen how badly I wanted it and she wasn't giving an inch. 'We don't do discounts here. If you want it, then buy it. If you don't want it, then go. You say it's tatty, but all that leafing through you've been doing will just make it even more so.' I felt everyone's eyes on me, and so reluctantly I got out five yuan and 80 cents, threw it down, then fled.

That night, I sat propped up in bed, perusing my book by the light of the bedside lamp. No one was stopping me. I am a thirty-year-old single man. The reason why I'm still single at thirty is because I haven't yet found a woman I'm interested in. As far back as I remember, my parents had separate bedrooms. Once, when I was ten years old, I got up in the night for a pee and saw a woman come out of my father's bedroom. She was wearing a diaphanous nightie, which hung open so that she was standing almost naked in front of me. She was clearly on the way to the toilet too. The light was too dim to see her features clearly but her nakedness struck me forcibly. It was my first sight of a female body. It was like glimpsing a dewdrop drifting through an ominously dark cloud. Her silvery nightie floated around her, revealing her flesh like a clam shell parting to show the clam inside, all fresh and satiny moist. But there was something that marred the overall effect: a tattoo that covered her chest and abdomen. It was a fish and a bird. A design from antiquity. It was grotesque – once seen, never forgotten. At the time, all I said was, rather brusquely: 'Who are you?' She did not answer, just smiled faintly and went into the bathroom. I waited for a long time outside in my pyjama bottoms and vest, but she did not emerge. Finally, I was so cold I scurried back to the bedroom I still shared with my mother. In the gloom, my mother was sitting up smoking a cigarette. I told her I'd had a nightmare, that I'd dreamt of a tattooed woman coming out of dad's room. She smiled grimly: 'You know who that was? She's a demon.' My hair stood on end.

In the twenty years since then, I have never forgotten my mother's words, and her strange expression. Her face, illuminated by the glow at the end of her cigarette, looked somehow malevolent. The demon, however, seemed to have lodged herself inside me. Compared to her, other women seemed insipid, like plain boiled water. The result was that I passed my entire youth undisturbed by desire. Except that every now and then I would wake up at dead of night and memories of the demon would come flooding back. It occurred to me that this rare and beautiful creature had disappeared off the face of the earth, and the thought plunged me into despair.

The book was tattered and filthy. But that did not prevent the words inside it drawing me in. The story was a historical one, and concerned an unsolved crime. Sometime in the 1820s, an American Navajo tribesman by the name of Ben walked into a bar, carrying an iron box. He and the bar owner, Al, were the best of friends and he passed the box over with the words: 'Al, mate, if I'm not back in three years, break the box open. When you've seen what's inside, you'll understand. But make sure you wait the full three years, otherwise a nasty accident might befall you.' And he set off on his trip. Al waited the full three years, resisting when everyone around him nagged him to open it, especially his wife, a beautiful flirtatious Sicilian. On the night that the three years were up, Al shut up his bar, ejecting all his customers, and carried the box into a backroom. Inside, he found only an envelope and, inside, a letter and a sheet of paper with three lines of figures written on it. The letter was obviously in Ben's handwriting and in it he wrote that when he was an explorer, he had once taken some soldiers out hunting with some other Indian tribespeople. They had been overtaken by bad weather and had followed a herd of antelope into the mountains, where they discovered a cave with a treasure trove inside, containing gold and gems worth ten million dollars. With the help of the Indians, they brought the treasure out and transferred it to a hidden location. The figures on the paper were code for the exact location and all the names of the group of hunters. If he, Ben, were not back in three years, the letter went on, that meant he had perished. He trusted Al, and was bequeathing the box to him, in the hopes that he could find the treasure and divide it into ten portions: one portion each for the families of the eight explorers, Al himself, and the person who managed to break the code. Al was thrilled. He set one of his waiters, Laurie, to work on breaking the code for him, but all their efforts proved fruitless. Right up until Al died, the code remained unbroken. Laurie's family, once quite well-off, fell on hard times but it was not until he was an old man that there was a breakthrough: he managed to crack the first line of code, by means of calculating the frequency with which certain words and numbers occurred in the Old Testament. That gave him the following:

I buried the treasure seven miles from Bells Canyon. For the exact location, see line three. The treasure comprises 5,091 pounds of gold, 3,876 pounds of silver, and an assortment of precious stones. It should be divided into ten portions…For the eight team members' addresses, see the second line.

Laurie was over the moon, but the second and third lines still evaded his every effort. The old man died in penury, but not before telling everyone his secret. For many generations thereafter, the best code-cracking brains, including computer experts, tried in vain to crack the code, employing computer calculations that would have taken a million people a billion years to perform using pen and paper. Finally, some bright spark made another breakthrough: the whole story of Ben and Al had come down to them through the words of Laurie. There were no independent witness accounts, of any kind, no documents, newspaper reports or wills. Even the box and the letter had gone. So the said bright spark inferred from this that the whole story had been one gigantic hoax perpetrated by Laurie, and there was no more to be said about the notorious code. But I still found the three lines of figures intriguing.

34, 151, 85, 217, 96, 952,
496, 89, 395, 28, 286, 16,
66, 203, 13, 745, 20, 138.

My mind raced whenever I conjured them up. First I speculated on the number 6. In the east, especially in China, it was a lucky number. Not so in the west, where it had sinister connotations, especially the triple, 666. Apparently, in the Book of Revelations, there was a warning about the Beast: any knowledgeable person could work out its name, 666. This mysterious pronouncement had Bible scholars and numerologists racking their brains. 6 in the Ancient World of the west was considered a perfect number, as was 28, because God created the world in six days, and the moon completed its cycle in 28 days. Now my leisure hours became much more entertaining – or rather, all my hours, because a lot of my time in the office was spent reading the newspapers, and that gave me time to work on these numbers. I did as Laurie had done and consulted all possible reference material. *The Declaration of Independence*, for example, and *On the Workings of the Universe*. But to no avail.

My boss organized a work trip out of China for a bunch of businessmen and women to drum up business. Each participant had to contribute 30,000 yuan, enough to cover a month in America. 30,000 yuan was nothing to them, it was peanuts. And my boss put me in charge of organizing the trip. It was not that she had particular trust in me, it was just that I was the only person in the company with any command of English. It took me two months to prepare, making the contacts, then sorting out passports and visas. I decided we would start our visit in a middle-sized town in the American West. It turned out to be idyllic. On arrival, my first impression was of a mass of brilliant blossoms. Every possible kind of flower covered the entire town. Tall trees and small shrubs were all in bloom, rambling and tumbling; a tidal wave of colour. The blossoms shone silver or gold in the sunlight, translucent, catching the light as if they were glass. The townsfolk strolled among the flowers with a serenity that was almost spiritual. As they saw us, they greeted us with a smile and a 'hello'. I discovered later that over 90% of the inhabitants were Mormons, and that Mormonism was a branch of Christianity that revered goodness and beauty. On my first day in town I met a Mormon missionary, a tall handsome young man who made it his business to convert me from the moment we met. With a smile on his face, he said that human life was so full of hardship that we all needed to be supported by the strength of eternal love. I asked how he knew that God existed. Through prayer, he declared. If you prayed repeatedly, the Lord would answer your prayers. After communing with the Lord, you would feel a peace and tranquillity and confidence and comfort that you had never felt before. I asked him how to pray, and he said it was simple:

1. Our Heavenly Father
2. Thank you for giving me your guidance (love, help, care…)
3. Please protect me…(telling one's most painful innermost truths)

 4. In Jesus's name, I pray for your protection. Amen

I followed his method and said several prayers, just out of curiosity. I really wanted to know how the Lord would answer. Mainly I prayed for two things: one, I hoped the Lord would help me find a woman I was interested in. That is, one like the demon I had seen as a child; and, two, that the Lord would help me break the legendary code, and thus work a miracle. But nothing happened. Of course, I had to pray in some horrible places, seeing as I had to get away from my associates and be well out of sight of my boss. I ended up shutting myself in the toilet at dead of night, places like that. Several times, I told my young missionary friend that I couldn't go on doing this. He just smiled and told me not to worry, the Lord was at my side. Then he said: 'Why don't we go and pray in Bells Canyon this weekend?' I was struck dumb. When I finally managed to get some words out, I said stupidly: 'How did you know about Bells Canyon?' He smiled again (he was always smiling): 'Bells Canyon is about seven or eight miles from my home, we go there a lot on holidays. Of course I know it.' I knew I had to keep my lips sealed; that I had to keep mum about my secret and the chance I was hoping to take. But he was right: the Lord really was with me.

That evening I discovered a secret passage. It actually started in the bathroom. Behind the cistern there was a loose tile. I pried it out, and like a Rubik's cube, found another tile was loose. One by one, I took them out, until I had uncovered a cavity. Without a moment's hesitation, I squeezed through. A damp earthy smell enveloped me. I remembered one thing very clearly: it was seven miles from here to Bells Canyon. I vowed that I would not keep even one precious stone for myself. My aim was not to get rich, but to perform a miracle. The sound of my own footsteps terrified me, but perhaps I was mistaken, and there were no footsteps… I had not felt my feet touch the ground for a long time. I seemed to be floating along in a cold damp miasma. The cavern was very deep. Thank heavens that I was enveloped in pitch darkness, because if I had been able to see the depths dropping away beneath my feet, I would no doubt have been scared out of my wits. I probably floated along in this manner for half an hour before my feet touched the ground. I took out my lighter and struck a flame: I saw I was surrounded by rocky outcrops, rust-coloured as if made of scorched metal. Perhaps the rock was from an ancient meteorite. I tried to shift the rocks but none of them would budge, despite my best efforts. They were stuck fast in the earth, or rather, it would be truer to say that the floor was made of stone. The whole cave was only about thirty square metres. It was a wide-open space with no nooks or crannies where treasure could lie hidden. However, I obviously wasn't going to give up. Anywhere I could reach I searched the rock walls with my fingers, but it was one complete slab without even a fragment broken off. My lighter gave only a dim light, and the flame flickered feebly in the damp air that arose from the floor. I was so desperate that I sent up another prayer to 'our Heavenly Father'. I held my palms together in front of my chest and shut my eyes tightly in an attitude of utmost devotion. Then a soft ray of light fell across my face. I opened my eyes. The light was coming from somewhere in the roof above me, to my left, like the light that filters through the stained glass windows of a church.

Still, I could see no treasure. The ray of light fell on the wall, as if to prompt me to shift my attention in that direction, and I suddenly realized that there was an enormous painting on the wall. The gentle light illuminated it as if it came from the hand of God. It was a beautiful wall painting, coloured in white, black and brown and composed of a group of beautiful black slaves escorting a fine lady to a celebration. The lady was drawn very big, in fluid, concise strokes. She held a candle in one hand and a bow in the other. She had brown skin and black hair, and wore strings of pearls around her wrists and ankles. But it was not her appearance that startled me, it was the realization that the woman's chest and belly were tattooed with eye-catching fish and bird designs, like hieroglyphs. They were the exact same designs as I remembered seeing on the woman, the beautiful demon, who had emerged from my father's bedroom and stayed etched in my memory ever since. The painting was uniquely creative. I stood transfixed, staring at the figure of the woman, but I could not make out her features very clearly, just a hazy outline from the light that fell from above, though even the outline was beautiful. The flame from her candle was carved in the form of three blooms, which resembled hyacinths or white roses. The background was painted all over with grapevines, leaves and more flowers. The fish and bird designs gave the impression of being transparent. It was as if candles had been placed at the back, so that they glittered like gold leaves in the darkness. I called a soft greeting to the woman, longing to see her float down from the wall as if in a fairy tale. But her tall figure remained exactly where it was, baring the tattoos on her abdomen before me. And then the ray of light gradually faded.

I told the Mormon missionary about the secret cave but, to my amazement, he evinced no surprise at all. He carried on smiling just as before as he listened patiently to my tale. I was so excited that I babbled on incoherently until finally I ran out of things to say. The missionary asked if I had finished, and I nodded. 'Then come with me,' he said. 'I'll take you somewhere, if you have nothing else on.' So I asked for the day off. The boss gave me a dirty look, probably thinking I wasn't due any holiday, but she did not dare offend me, because I was the ears and lips of the entire delegation, at least on this occasion, and who knew if there would be a subsequent one? In any case, I didn't care. I just kept my eyes on my mysterious smiling missionary and followed him through the streets. The streets were quiet and warm, the fragrance of the flowers cutting out the city noise. We walked into a square with a garden in the middle and on the other side I saw an immense library. We went up in the lift, to the 11th floor. A man came up to the missionary and whispered in his ear, turned and greeted me politely, then said to a young woman sitting behind a glass door: 'K603, please.' I imagined this was the catalogue number of a book. The young woman swiftly keyed in a series of numbers on her computer and another glass door opened, delivering a thick hard-bound book on a conveyor belt. Its name was *Rock Paintings of the World and the Rock Painting World*. It was filled with colour plates and black and white illustrations of rock paintings from Altamira in Spain and Lascaux in France, as well as Norway, Finland, Siberia, India and South-East Asia, Japan and North and South Africa, right the way to Wandjina art from Australia, and American tribal rock art. The Mormon turned to a page and there before me was the painting I had seen in the cave. The caption read: Discovered by three Germans in 1918, on Brandberg Mountain, Namibia, South-West Africa. As if that wasn't enough, there was another line below which read: 'The painting shows a negro prince going hunting.' Good heavens, how could such a beautiful woman be a prince? To my further astonishment I realized that her tattoos had vanished, and there were no bird and fish designs to be seen at all. My mouth dropped open. 'Isn't this the painting you were describing?' my missionary friend asked. I shook my head, completely bemused. Eventually, I pulled myself together: 'No, there must be some mistake,' I said.

That evening, I took the missionary to our accommodation, ignoring the boss's dirty looks. I led him into the bathroom and locked the door behind us, deaf to the boss's thundering knocking. But we searched in vain for the loose tile. It was nowhere to be found. Driven to fury by the missionary's unchanging smile, I attacked the urinal, smashing it to pieces. But none of the tiles budged an inch. Finally the missionary's patient smile was exhausted. He let himself out and departed, with the words: 'You need to pray a bit harder. You're still a long way from the Lord.' I followed him out, and the boss glared angrily at me. 'When we get back to China, you'll pay for this,' she said.

Now I lay in bed leafing through the book, which was growing tattier by the minute. Just as I had foreseen, I had been given the sack. But I did not feel that it had affected me badly. I believed the evidence of my own eyes. I was convinced I could crack the last two lines of the code. One day a celestial light would shine on me, just like the ray of light from that indeterminate spot on the roof of the cave, gentle and warm. I switched on the lamp, drew the curtains and shut the remaining light of evening out. Suddenly there was a ring at the doorbell. The girl from next door came in. She was a foolish creature, and although she was the only female of my acquaintance, I did not like her at all. She was forever taking books from my bookshelf and not returning them, and when she did bring them back, they did not look like the same books. She mangled them so badly it was hard to tell whether she had been eating them or reading them. What's more, I felt I had to lend her books because her uncle was a third-rate author. Tonight she had come late, and unusually for her, didn't pick a fight with me, just covered her mouth with her hand and laughed. 'How strange! You read books like this too?' I glared at her: 'What do you mean "books like this"? I don't believe for a moment that you understand a word of it!' She burst out laughing, and the noise echoed off the walls as she laughed and laughed, on and on, until she was bent double clutching her belly. Finally, she sputtered out: 'My uncle would be tickled pink hearing you say that! He wrote it.' I was gobsmacked. Then I insisted: 'It's obviously a translation! Look, the name of the American author's here: John Kinsky!' She laughed louder than ever. 'You're such a fool! That's never his real name! My uncle can call himself what he wants, John Kinsky or John Kennedy!' I was pouring with sweat by this time but I wasn't giving up. 'But what about those three lines of text? What's that all about? You know, I really did go to Bells Canyon and seven kilometres from there I found a cave.' She gave me a queer look and stopped laughing. 'Are you OK?' she asked. 'Feel your forehead, have you got a temperature? I'm telling you, I was the one who wrote that code, I just scribbled down the first thing that came into my head. How did you find a cave based on that rubbish?' She said a bit more, then she left, leaving me all alone in the dimly lit room. I switched off the lamp and got out my lighter. I seemed to be transported back to that cave with its enormous rock painting. In the pale blue flame, I let my imagination roam free. At least here and now I was free to think.

BLACK WATERFALL

An old man is slowly making his way up the mountain.

The hottest, most insufferable part of the day has passed but his skin is slick with sweat. Not that he seems flustered; on the contrary, he appears cool, unruffled. He is dressed in a flowing summer robe and, viewed from afar, exudes an almost otherworldly aura. Glittering rays of evening sunlight spill out from behind him. There's something in his hand. Something bright.

The dark mountain seems to move with him as he climbs, as though about to squash him. He keeps a steady pace but this steadiness is unnerving. The mountain is behind him and he looks as though he's carrying it on his back. His footsteps are at once light and very heavy.

A little stream glimmers at his feet. This stream has a beautiful name. It has flowed for many, many years yet no one has ever traced it to its source.

Legend has it that men have tried. But the only one ever to make it back said that he had found himself at the bottom of a rocky crevasse, where he lost his way. The little stream was suddenly hundreds of little streams, coursing down the sheer rock face like an upside-down coral tree with hundreds of snow-white branches. Beautiful, certainly, but enough to send a person mad.

This was where the other men had carried on, delirious, never to be seen again.

The one who made it back was revered as a sage. After his return, he lived a long and solitary life on this very mountain. His white beard grew long enough to brush the floor and, when his time came, he died a peaceful death, without any illness.

Everyone loved to listen to his stories. He said, 'For those who make it to the crevasse, there awaits a sight to behold.' And people believed every word he said, for his beard was more majestic than any they had ever seen.

Later, a sign was erected – here, at this juncture in the path.

As a result, the area developed. Some bright spark put up an awning and chiselled some stone tables and benches, engraving them with mysterious designs, a little like the taotie motifs you might find on ancient bronze artefacts. Who knows if those man-eating beasts, all head, no body, ever really existed? If not, how did anyone ever think them up? But then again, if so, how did anyone ever escape to tell the tale? Either way, it's ancient history. A long, long time ago. No one is seeking to verify their existence; they simply revere them as divine.

The awning has been there for generations. Nowadays, it's a jaunty red-white-blue affair, like something you might see featured in a foreign magazine. Next to it, there's a little stand stocked with beer and soft drinks. The young woman selling them is too haggard to be called attractive, but her hair – well, her hair is truly beautiful. It's not permed or styled in any particular way. She might have just washed it: it's damp and hanging loosely over shoulders. It looks heavy, as if it would be too thick to comb. And it's exceptionally black. So black it hardly seems real.

She wears a cerise jacket over a pair of loose black trousers and is made up just like all the other wives on the mountain. But there's something about her appearance that sets her apart. A certain, intangible charm.

The man crouched to the side of the stand must be her husband. His jowls are fleshy squares, jiggling slightly as he stares vacantly into the distance. His whole being looks chiselled out of stone; as square and solid as one of the tables. To carry beer and soft drinks up such a high mountain, day in, day out – that takes some doing.

There's only a handful of customers, all city folk. Two of them are girls. Pretty ones, each sporting an enormous pair of sunglasses, the lenses shaped like big black butterflies. Those kinds of butterflies are not good omens; there's a legend about that, too.

At the sight of the glasses, the young woman at the stand freezes, as though suddenly remembering something. Then she lolls back across the counter, alongside a black feather duster.

It is at this moment that the old man walks slowly into the shelter.

Up close, his billowing, otherworldly robe is old and threadbare. The faint outline of his protruding rib cage is visible through the fabric. Fluttering against his ribs, the fabric resembles a very old, very thin sheet of yellowing paper, ready to snag and rip at any moment. The shiny object in his hand turns out to be a walking stick. It is topped with an ivory handle, its creamy veins polished to a high gleam. The handle and the shaft are linked by a loop of dark gold, which glimmers like a flame in the dusky twilight.

'Looks like gold,' comments one of the city boys. The group starts to discuss it.

The old man sits on a stone bench, both hands resting on the stick, his eyes squinted against the light. No one can guess his age, but they all sense something odd about the wrinkles on his face – they meander like the little stream, with no discernible source. And, like the growth rings of a gnarled old tree, each line seems to have its own story. The oddest thing of all is how these wrinkles overwhelm his features, to the point that he barely seems to have any expression at all.

'Is that man crying or laughing?' The black feather duster on the counter moves, revealing a little duck egg of a face. It's a little girl. A skinny thing, bearing a close resemblance to the woman. What seemed to be a duster is, of course, her hair. As black as the woman's, only nowhere near as clean and tidy.

The woman does not reply. She is still lolling across the counter. Her beautiful hair falls in a heavy curtain over her shoulders, obscuring most of her face, spilling over her arms. It pools around her like ink.

The old man spots a young woman in a cerise jacket, and his wrinkles twitch. He pulls a white porcelain bottle from his trouser pocket, strokes it, then pulls out the stopper. A fruity whiff of alcohol. He takes a hearty gulp, smacks his lips, and instantly seems revived; even his wrinkles lessen a little.

'Maotai,' says one of the boys, sniffing the air.

'No way,' says another, shaking his head. 'Nowadays that stuff's only for big shot banquets. Even on the black market, it's crazy expensive.' He waves his hand. 'You really think this guy has that kind of money?'

'Hey, don't judge a dumpling by its wrapper! For all you know, he could be loaded. Isn't it the fashion these days, for big deal officials to put on poor clothes and go travelling about?'

'Bullshit! What kind of official goes about without at least two bodyguards in tow? At most, this guy's an archaeologist or hydrology expert, something like that. He's never been successful in his whole life, but he's making the most of the time he has left and getting out a bit.'

'Maybe he's an artist. Look at those brooding eyes!'

'You talk such crap! He's just an ordinary old man, probably had a fight with his wife or something. You see? He had a bit to drink, and now his forehead's all shiny.'

'He seems kind of addicted, he's not done yet.'

They glance over again, mouths pursed in disapproval.

The old man is half listening. He's only taking tiny sips of the wine, although it's true that his forehead is shiny. And his eyes may be brooding, but they're bright. Come a little closer, and you'll see the boyish mischief still lurking in those dark brown irises. His left hand holds the bottle and all five fingers of his right hand are cupped protectively around it, guarding it tightly, stroking up and down the outside. Buffing the white porcelain until it shines.

'Hey, Mister, how about a bottle of beer? It's good stuff, brought up from the city,' calls the stone table man. His tone is gloomy. He's smoking some kind of cheap cigarette. Keeps puffing out clouds of smoke. Now he seems less like a stone table and more like a copper incense burner.

The old man shakes his head.

'Well, if no beer, how about some cake? You've a long way ahead of you!' The stone table (or incense burner) isn't ready to give in.

The old man waves off the suggestion. He puts away the bottle and pulls some foil-wrapped chocolate from his pocket. The girls with the butterfly glasses have sharp eyes, and note that it's the dark, low-sugar kind. The old man's hand trembles slightly as he breaks off a small piece and places it in his mouth.

Cautiously, the little girl approaches him.

A skinny thing, dressed in a cerise jacket and trousers. Most likely made from her mother's leftover fabric. But the jacket's too short and rises up her tummy, exposing the dirty rings running all around it; it seems a while since she last had a bath. The corners of her eyes are crusty. She looks like her mother, except a prettier version. Cleaned up a bit, she'd be a match for any of those pretty city girls.

She stares for a while at the dark black contents of the old man's mouth, then starts sucking her fingers.

The old man's mouth twists into a smile. Once again, the wrinkles on his face are like the stream, twisting and turning as it flows. He breaks off another piece of chocolate and holds it under the girl's nose.

'It smells good! What's this candy called?' The girl sniffs, then reaches hesitantly for it. Her black eyes are wide, staring at the old man.

A spark of warmth flares in his narrowed eyes. Followed by a flicker of sadness. A pause, and then he puts a hand to the side of his mouth, puffs out twice, and pats the girl lightly on her bare tummy, smiling. This time it's a broad smile, revealing two rows of surprisingly healthy white teeth.

The girl smiles back, showing off her two rows of little black teeth.

'Come back over here, young lady!' yells the stone table, making everybody jump. The girl's hand shakes and the chocolate falls to the ground. Her mouth turns down and she turns to her mother, eyes brimming with tears, as though waiting for approval before letting them fall.

'Do you have to yell like that over such a tiny thing?' says her mother, addressing the man. 'She's only little!'

But before she can finish, her husband's fist slams down angrily on the counter, rocking the steelyard and the abacus.

'Don't get me started on you! Didn't I tell you to get some sleep last night? But no, you stayed up washing that great lump of flesh of yours. Now your eyes look ready to roll out of your head, and you're lazing around napping. If we don't sell all this by the end of the day, you're carrying it down, not me!'

The woman lifts her head, letting her dark hair cascade down her back. On her face, faint patches of butterfly-shaped pigment leap about as she talks.

'Let the customers make up their own minds! You can't go round speaking to them like this. Maybe we annoy you, but this nice old gentleman here just offered our little one a bit of his candy. Is that so wrong? I tell you, if you want people to stop coming, you're going the right way about it!'

Unsurprisingly, a couple of the slightly older city boys get up and walk off. The others sit rooted to the spot, as though watching a band of performing monkeys.

The husband lowers his voice. 'Nice old gentleman? That old geezer! What kind of candy do you call that, anyway? Black as a goddamn goat. If he can't even spare a bit of change for a drink, what the hell use is he?'

The old man is still sipping slowly at his bottle, although the glow has faded from his eyes and forehead.

The girl goes back up to him and starts fiddling with his belongings. They're all so novel to her. She reaches for his stick, which is leaning against the bench, but the moment she touches it, his head jerks up as though electrocuted and he snatches it back. He grips it with both hands, not drinking now, and rests his chin wearily on top. A few puffs of white hair hang down over his eyes, blowing gently in the breeze.

The woman suddenly stops talking, her eyes going wide. They're as black as her daughter's, although nowhere near as bright. The old man doesn't look at her. He isn't looking at anyone; his gaze soars past the dark crest of the mountain, as though seeing through to a world on the other side.

The stream is golden in the twilight, each pebble inside it a dazzling gemstone. In these waters, perhaps you really could pan for gold. Otherwise, why would anyone have given it such a beautiful name? When the ancients named something, they always had their reasons.

The little girl opens and closes her mouth, as though saying something. The old man slowly withdraws his eyes from the distance and smiles at her. But it's different to before. He feels a tightening in his chest, and his smile darkens.

The little girl picks up her dropped chocolate and puts it in her mouth. As she chews, her face contorts oddly, as though she's not quite sure what it is that she's tasting. But afterwards she draws her lips back into a grin, revealing her little black teeth.

Her parents are yelling again. By the time they finish, the light has faded and the travellers have dispersed.

The old man stands up, leaning on his stick. He's stiff, but there's that same unhurried steadiness to his pace. That odd, unnerving steadiness. Before long, he's quite some way from the awning.

'I can't believe it! He's made it to the boundary sign!' exclaims the woman, shouting with incredulity now, rather than anger. Her eyes are trained on his retreating figure.

'And? He won't make it past, you'll see,' says her husband, his anger also eased. He too stares fixedly at the old man, watching him as he pauses in front of the sign. On it is written: 'Danger, do not proceed. For Thousand Pine Ridge, please head east.'

No one has ever gone beyond the sign.

Their eyes are round with shock. The man's mouth hangs open, exhaling the foul odour of a sluggish digestion.

The old man's stick resolutely crosses the boundary. His pace remains steady. The couple starts shouting at once.

'Mister! Stop! You can't walk there! It's too dangerous, come back!'

The woman's bright cerise jacket and long black hair flicker and flash in the remaining twilight, joining the flickers of the stream. The old man does not look back.

The twilight fades as the sun sets behind the mountain, turning its dark mass into a looming silhouette. The stream becomes a multi-coloured ribbon, the underwater pebbles no longer gemstones so much as sunken bursts of dye.

The stone table man heads down the mountain. The little girl is fast asleep. All is calm. The woman stares at the distant sign until her vision starts to blur. The old man has not come back! She turns away and lets out a loud yawn.

An enormous black butterfly flutters past. A bad omen! Despite her tiredness, she can still conjure the thought. It is now that she sees the old man, in sharp relief. He seems to be following the butterfly.

That butterfly is as black as my hair, she thinks. The only difference is that its feelers have golden tips, like crowns. As she watches the butterfly, she feels a curl of fear. It is following the stream, darting here and there to sniff wildflowers and grasses on either bank, then swooping in close to the water.

It's admiring its reflection! Its outline is clearly reflected in the stream, the two spots of gold floating on the surface, big then small, bright then dark. The woman thinks to herself how long it's been since she looked in a mirror.

The old man keeps on walking, slowly shaking off the mountain behind him. He heaves a great sigh, then pulls out his bottle and takes a couple of sips. The moss on the rocks by the stream is growing thicker and is slippery beneath his stick. Inside his loose, flapping trousers, his skinny legs are trembling. But he keeps on, one step at a time. *How much longer does he have left?* thinks the woman.

She notices some pink and white flowers growing along the stream. The old man stops but doesn't pick them. He must not have any granddaughters to pick them for. She makes a mental note of the location. Such beautiful flowers.

The first stars are out. No moon. Perhaps it's blocked by the mountain. The night-time chill is slowly chasing away the heat of the day. The old man steadily follows those two spots of gold. The butterfly is so big, so black, its wings like black velvet curtains – they must be hiding something.

The path grows more treacherous, yet the old man picks his way with apparent ease. The woman looks at the darkened sky. The pale green moonlight. The silvery trees. So beautiful! No one would believe it! Who would believe that the trees could dye the moon green, and that the moon could make the trees gleam silver? What a wonderful place it is, on the other side of the sign. When she has time, she resolves to leave her grumpy old husband alone for a bit and take her daughter over for a look. She almost feels like laughing. The old man seems just as fascinated by the silver trees as she is: he's walking around and around them, knocking off fruits with his stick. She recognises a pear tree and thinks darkly that these non-mountain people just don't understand – at this time of year, pears will still be sour.

The big black butterfly is slowing down. Perhaps it's getting tired, too. Its beating wings are as large as a bat's. The black of the night does not mask them, for they are blacker still. She fears for this old gentleman's fate. In these parts, such a butterfly is the stuff of legend; no one has ever seen one in real life. *To what does he owe this misfortune!* she frets, her hair rustling against her pillow.

Somehow, the old man is speeding up, the butterfly close by his side. His head is lowered, and his skinny legs are barely wider than his stick, giving the impression that he has three legs. The woman bites her lip, unsure whether to laugh or cry.

The three legs come to an abrupt halt. They cannot proceed any farther. The woman widens her eyes, jet-black but not so bright as they once were. She can feel her hair blowing against her face, inky as the night.

A sheer rock face rises before the old man. So high, so steep. So calmly blocking the way, like an expanse of silence. Like a stone city wall rising from a desert. The woman feels her heart lurch, as though falling from a great height.

The old man is also stunned. They stand there for a while, in silent opposition: him and the city wall. Moonlight spills across it, thick as milk. Faces seem to be carved into the surface; hundreds and hundreds of faces. The old man observes them in silence, pulling back every so often, his brow creasing with surprise. It seems to be full of old friends. The woman also observes the faces, but they change every time she blinks. Another one, then another one, and some of them are crying real tears.

Only when she looks more closely, those aren't tears at all: they are hundreds of tiny streams, running down the cliff face. Just like a gleaming white coral tree hanging upside down. Just like the legend says, twisting and turning like a labyrinth, confusing all who lay eyes on them. The old man is still following that butterfly, jamming his stick into fissures in the rock, hauling himself up.

'Mister! You'll never make it! That butterfly's a bad omen!' she screams, and is shaken awake by her husband, lying by her side.

'It's the middle of the night, what's all this fuss about! You're itching for a beating, is that it?'

The woman drapes her cerise jacket over her shoulders and goes to stand by the window. A night like any other. No green moonlight, no silvery trees.

The old man feels himself transform into an old ape. He thrusts his stick into a crack, grips it with both hands, pulls himself up, then ascends to the next one. He suddenly realises that he is not old; in comparison to this rock, he has barely been born. His life, all his heavy burdens, they are but a flash in time. The things that he has seen today, no one will ever believe. He should show them. As he thinks this, the mischief returns to his irises and he feels a hot ball of energy gather in his rib cage. He can't let it go to waste. To say nothing of the big black butterfly still flying delicately ahead, opening and closing those velvety wings, stirring the wind. With every flap, it sheds a few grains of frosty powder. At one point, it flies right up him, its wing knocking against his ear. He glimpses an eye, which flashes a sinister green. It's a painful knock, accompanied by a low-pitched buzz. It unsettles him. Can this really be a butterfly? It's so big, it seems more like a bat.

He perches on a branch protruding from the rock. It strikes him as comical, like a return to childhood. His mother gazing up at him from the ground. Above is the sky, full of pink stars, close enough to touch. Below is an expanse of black. Presumably still full of trees. Trees, but not his mother. The trees might not tower over him any longer, but they are still majestic. A crowd of majestic dwarfs. He chuckles to himself.

Continuing, he finally reaches the very last crack. He stares blankly. There is nothing. The rock is blank. The stream seems to have entered into it. Straining his eyes, he can see intermittent bursts of something glistening beneath the moss.

He thought of everything. The only thing he did not consider was: *what if there is nothing.*

His eyelids itch; something's rubbing against his face. Snapping his eyes wide open, he finds himself staring straight into a dark green eye at the centre of an enormous black wing. His grizzled hair stands on end. He frantically waves his stick, whipping it through the blackness, watching it bend into an arc of light. The big black wing glistens in the darkness.

There is nothing!

He becomes aware that he's lying face-down on the ground. His chin is slimy with moss. He has the vague sensation that his body is gradually turning to stone, while his soul shudders along on a mountain breeze, at one with the lonely echoes of the valley, and the distant roar of the ocean waves.

Stars drift easily through the night sky, clustering together and then parting again, arranging and rearranging themselves like the view through a kaleidoscope. Colliding, shattering into crystalline dust particles and then receding into the deepest depths of the cosmos. One star even lands on him. Pink, not heavy at all. Like a beautiful, translucent, star-shaped balloon. It bounces a few times. A little while later, it turns into a series of round pink bubbles. The entire universe is slowly shifting, drifting like a thin, thin cloud, covering his body.

A dribble of ice-cold water. The stream is seeping from underneath the moss. A strand of black hair floats in it, like a long black fish tail. So supple, so elegant in its flexing, calling out to be touched – and looking ready to flick water in the face of anyone who dares to try.

The old man sees a young woman in the stream, watching him.

Bring me back to life, I promise I...

The woman from the refreshment stand hears a loud rumbling in the darkness and reaches for her daughter.

'What is it, Mummy?' says the girl, confused.

'Thunder!' replies the woman, raising her eyes to the awning. Every so often, rat droppings fall off it. Her husband usually suspends their food in hanging baskets, and notices if they're down by so much as a single chili. He drinks. When he drinks, he gets violent. He'll throw his wife and child to the floor and tread all over them, as though stepping on old dishrags. When he's drunk, he squats under the awning, eyes wide and vacant, smoking one cheap cigarette after another. Who knows what he's thinking.

The woman notices a sudden burst of very bright light.

Perhaps that rumbling isn't thunder, after all.

She looks in the direction of the crevasse. The noise is coming from the rock face.

What is it? What on earth is it?

The old man lies there in the moss, not moving. Panicked, the woman tries to shout him awake. 'Mister, the moss is freezing! Wake up!'

The old man stirs, then stirs again. His eyes slowly open. They are big and bright; a young person's eyes. Limpid as the water in the stream. So still that they reflect the moon, the sky, the far-off stars; so wide that they seem about to swallow it all down. The eyelashes are moist, and there's a big, bright point of light concentrated to one side of the pupils – but after a while it falls away, and is gone.

The old man is crying! She feels her own eyes prickle. A big black wing is obstructing her view, like a curtain; she can't see a thing. But what does the old man see?

The deafening rumble is getting farther away. Her daughter jerks awake. 'Mummy, there's thunder!'

So such sublime waterfalls do still exist! This is the source of that deafening boom! In the darkness, water crashes down and then rises ten thousand feet high, like coils of smoke. It's so ancient, so majestic, so abundant! Standing before it, how could he be anything other than a child. Glassy droplets spray against his face as he rises from the moss-covered ground. He is childishly giddy. The waterfall churns up mist, clear as air, looking like it would vanish with one wave of his walking stick.

At long last, he has seen it. It is here, before his eyes – no wonder it has inspired such a tale, and no wonder so many others have chosen to believe it and come all this way to chase it, even at the expense of their lives.

A young woman is standing behind the waterfall, her pitch black hair making it shine black. It is like the first time he saw her, her hair as thick and inky as the night, imbued with all the lightness of a dream. His beautiful young bride did not die; an older woman drove her away while he was sleeping. Drove her away and replaced her, because she thought she could fool him, and that he would be too cowardly to protest. She cheated him. Cheated them. That generation. But today, he has found her. She's there. His bride.

Her long black hair floats and flickers behind the waterfall. So she's the queen of this stone city. He's relieved, asks a hundred questions, but all she does is smile and wave, inviting him to enter. This waterfall is the gateway to her, and once he enters, it will be even more spectacular. He walks eagerly into the beaded curtain of water, only to feel the sudden force of ten thousand steel blades driving into him, leaving his body in tatters. *The gateway to hell*, he thinks.

He finds himself in another world. He has never seen such a perfect karst cave before. A crystalline palace. It feels prehistoric. Stalactites of all sizes hang from the ceiling like ice lanterns, or like shafts of coral agate, thick as pillars, fine as hairs, fleeting as racing horses, still as hunting tigers, taking on weird and wonderful hues in accordance with the light. His bride's black hair is blowing on the wind, releasing a clear, penetrating scent. He examines the walls of the cave. There are no carvings or ancient totems, but the rock face alone is enough to spark his imagination, like watching the infinite shifting of clouds in a summer sky.

Suddenly, he's aware of something soft beneath his feet. He looks down, and it's a snake. Emerald green. It looks a little like the bamboo-leaf viper you find in more southern parts. Looking around, he sees that the rock face is actually a writhing mass of snakes. He does not panic. At this point, a monster with a snake's body and man's face could appear – or a monster with a pig's body and a man's face – and he would not be frightened. He feels a strong sense of calm. He isn't even following her any more – that beautiful young bride that he once loved so much. He will not follow anyone anymore. He walks alone. As he wishes. He recalls those drifting stars above the crevasse. Each one on a trajectory of its own.

He loses his stick.

He searches everywhere. He sees what looks like a wing of that big black butterfly, but when he looks more closely, it's an old woman standing in the cave. Her black gown trails on the ground. She scowls angrily from a thickly-powdered white face. That scowl is very familiar. Usually, he turns solemn at the sight of it, facing the wall like a scolded child. But today, he is not bowing to anyone. The scowling woman starts to reprimand him, jabbering on and on. He does not want to listen; he cannot. He feels as high above it all as the waterfall. The woman becomes increasingly angry and spits pearly strings of sticky black mucus.

How did such beautiful black hair transform into such venom?

As he ponders this question, his thoughts turn to the ancient story of the owl. He recalls very little of this nocturnal creature and its long-ago adventures, other than that it could change shape, transforming into all kinds of alluring characters. But he will be enticed no longer. He will take charge and use this creature for his own ends, progressing to the pinnacle of all beauty. He wants to bellow with laughter at the thought. None of this will have been in vain: from this moment forth, he will be a new man. No more fear, no more fleeing. He will not cheat and nor will he be cheated. He will live out his remaining days doing just as his heart desires.

The waterfall plunges into the depths of the night. It cares nothing for the suffering of men. In a sudden cool wave, the old man feels every cell of his body rinsed clean.

He gazes at the waterfall. There seems to be black hair surging inside it. The water is gradually reddening, and he understands that daybreak is approaching – he spins around, to see that the dawn has stained the walls of the cave red, too. He strolls out, without any qualms at all. The deafening boom quietens, until silence is all around him. The waterfall is a red silk curtain, billowing down from the sky, ten thousand feet high. A flock of mountain birds, cawing mournfully, dives into the clouds. There are hundreds of thousands of multi-coloured butterflies, dancing on the breeze. He might have glimpsed the big black butterfly, in among the splendour. Perhaps it wasn't an owl he was thinking of before, but the golden crow that lives in the sun? As he considers this, the sun spills into the sky. Such magnificence is beyond description. He trembles, then booms with laughter, completely forgetting his disappeared stick. His laughter is infectious, for at the sound of it, the birds, the butterflies, the snakes – all creatures near and far – dance for joy. And he feels himself gradually merging with them, aware that this is the crowning moment of his whole entire life, the greatest joy known to man: he will die without regrets.

That sign still stands halfway up the mountain, warning away all the climbers that come across it. That man still hauls cold drinks up to the awning, day in, day out. He earns a bit of money, then he drinks, then he gambles, then he rages. His wife still lies wearily across her counter, fighting to keep her eyes open. But now her pitch-black hair is tied back in a bun, which weighs heavily on the back of her head. The butterfly markings on her face are even more pronounced. The little girl, that skinny thing with hair as black as her mother's, still sneaks up to charm food out of travellers, sure that other people's snacks must surely be tastier than hers. She skips and jumps about, impervious to her mother's scolding, unaware that soon she will have a little brother, who will come to vie with her food and clothes.

Early one evening, something happens to shatter the routine: the little girl sees something glittering in the stream, and yells, 'Gold!

Mummy, there's gold in the water!'

Her father rushes over, the travellers rush over – only her mother, that young woman in the cerise jacket, is left behind, still lolling with her head propped on her hands, watching from afar.

When they fish it out, it's a walking stick. Below the ivory handle, there's a loop of gold. *The old man*, thinks the girl's father. He tests it in his hands; it's heavy. The travellers are clustered around. One busybody insists they should report it to the local authorities. The man glares at him and grips the stick with all his might, as though trying to lift it, but his usual iron strength is no use at all; the stick will not budge.

'There's something inside!' he shouts to his wife, redoubling his efforts, his face bathed in sweat. He runs to the counter and grabs the big axe he uses to chop wood, ignoring his wife's protests as he hacks into the shaft.

It splits open. Inside, it is empty aside from a bunch of black hair. It seems to have been there a long time. As soon as it is exposed to the air, it shrivels up as though on fire. An instant and it's gone, vanished in a puff of smoke.

Nicky Harman translated A Celestial Voice, A Classic Tragedy, Pompom, Marrying Out and The Story of a Secret Key.

Natascha Bruce translated Miss Asia, Silver Shield, Yellow Peace Rose, The Art Gallery and Black Waterfall.